fe and
ound
Cultu

Riders of the Barren Plains

Jeff Steed rode into Carmon looking for work, but when he got caught up in a bank raid he found himself running from both Sheriff Cassidy Yates and the bank raider Blake Kelly. To escape from the net that was inexorably closing in on him he assumed the identity of a dead man. But as that man was the leader of a supply convoy, he had to undertake a hazardous journey across the Barren Plains to the silver miners at Bleak Point.

With the convoy being escorted by the lawman who had been trying to catch him and the bandit he double-crossed hiding out in the Barren Plains, can Jeff ever hope to survive?

By the same author

The Outlawed Deputy
The Last Rider from Hell
Death or Bounty
Bad Day in Dirtwood
Devine's Law
Yates's Dilemma
The Ten Per Cent Gang
Mendosa's Gun-runners
Wanted: McBain
Six-shooter Bride
Dead by Sundown
Calhoun's Bounty
Calloway's Crossing
Bad Moon over Devil's Ridge
Massacre at Bluff Point
The Gallows Gang

Riders of the Barren Plains

I.J. Parnham

ROBERT HALE · LONDON

First published in Great Britain 2009

ISBN 978-0-7090-8768-7

Robert Hale Limited
Clerkenwell House
Clerkenwell Green
London EC1R 0HT

www.halebooks.com

Typeset by
Derek Doyle & Associates, Shaw Heath
Printed and bound in Great Britain by
CPI Antony Rowe, Chippenham and Eastbourne

CHAPTER 1

'Sorry, cowboy. I ain't got no work for you.'

'Obliged for your time,' Jeff Steed said, then shuffled off down the bar to stand beside his next target, a portly rancher.

The rancher put down his drink and turned. Before Jeff could even deliver his speech, he snapped out his decision.

'Like he said. I've got no work for you.'

'Obliged for—'

'You weren't listening.' The rancher looked Jeff up and down with undisguised contempt, taking in his threadbare clothing, caked-on grime, and holed boots. 'I've got no work for *you*.'

The rancher roared with laughter at his insult then turned away to order another drink.

'Obliged for your time,' Jeff said dutifully, then moved on.

When he'd ridden into Carmon, Jeff had been told that the local ranchers and trail bosses drank in this saloon, so if there was hiring to be done it'd happen here. But he'd had no luck.

Two days without food meant he'd had to hitch in his belt to its tightest hole to stop his stomach growling. Despite that his trousers were still loose, but he didn't have the energy to bore another hole. He had to find work soon and he didn't like to think what would happen if he didn't.

Only one man was left at the end of the bar to try. He was drinking with a stern expression that said he had plenty on his mind and didn't want interruptions. Jeff still sidled up to him, but he was so dispirited he couldn't even summon up the words to ask his standard question. After he had stood there for several seconds, the man spoke up.

'So you're looking for work?' Although he stayed looking straight ahead, the question sent a tremor of hope fluttering in Jeff's empty guts.

'Sure,' Jeff said.

'I'm Blake Kelly,' the man said, lowering his voice. 'Ever heard of me?'

'Nope. Then again I ain't from around these parts, but I just want to say, I'll do anything.'

'Anything, eh?' Blake sipped his whiskey then turned to consider him. His steady gaze took in Jeff's tattered clothing as the previous man had. He licked his lips and a lively gleam in the eye softened his dour expression. 'I'm a man short so I have some work for a man who'll do *anything*.'

Jeff heard the emphasis, but his pride had snapped some time ago, so even the possibility of a disgusting, backbreaking task for little pay made his mouth water with anticipation.

'What'll you pay me?'

'Straight to the point. I like that.' Blake withdrew a handful of bills from his pocket. 'Twenty dollars for an hour's work, maybe two.'

'An hour!' Jeff spluttered. His heart beat faster, but then experience told him where this apparently lucrative offer would lead.

'Sure, and don't worry about getting paid. I'll give you ten dollars now and the rest on completion.' Blake winked. 'Provided you can find me.'

Jeff smiled as Blake read his mind, not that that would have been hard when he was so downtrodden.

'What is this job?'

'And finally the important question.' Blake beckoned for Jeff to join him in leaning on the bar then lowered his voice to a whisper. 'You stand on the corner of the road opposite the bank and look out for certain men. If you see them, you tell me.'

Jeff frowned. He was about to say he didn't want to get involved in any trouble, but his stomach provided an encouraging growl and from down the bar braying laughter sounded from the man who had sneered at him earlier.

'Which men?' he asked.

Blake placed a ten-dollar bill on the bar and pushed it towards him.

'Lawmen,' he said.

I'm sorry,' Sheriff Cassidy Yates said, 'I can't help you no more.'

Abigail Scott wailed, making several customers look at her before she lowered her head and poked at her steak in embarrassment for her outburst. Cassidy had brought her to Maud Tyler's Eatery, hoping the food and bustling atmosphere would soften the blow, but her watering eyes and failure to eat more than a mouthful of mashed beets told him that plan had failed.

'I'd heard you never gave up,' she murmured, her voice catching. 'Perhaps I heard wrong.'

Cassidy offered a smile. 'You didn't, but I've ignored my other duties by coming to Carmon. Now that every lead has turned up blank, I have to get back to Monotony. But if you learn something new. . . .'

She returned a small smile. 'I understand. I'll keep on looking and asking and searching. If I find out anything, I know where you are.'

Cassidy placed a hand on her arm and gripped it, then gestured at the food before he began eating. Taking his cue, she carved her steak.

Abigail's mission appeared straightforward, but it had confounded Cassidy. Her sister Jane and husband Ethan had gone West looking to put down roots, but she'd heard nothing from them. After three months of waiting for the news they'd promised to provide weekly, she'd become worried and had come to Carmon to search for them.

With Marshal McCoy being injured Cassidy had directed the search, but he hadn't found them, or even found any hint as to where they had gone. All he had to help him was Jane's last letter, which said they would take the train to Carmon. But nobody had seen them and after a week of roaming around he didn't even know for sure that they'd arrived here.

'Just keep your chin up,' he said between mouthfuls. 'People don't just disappear. Someone somewhere will know something.'

She narrowed her eyes. 'Does that mean you reckon that something bad has happened to them?'

'There's plenty of trouble around and two fresh faces stepping down off a train are likely targets for it, but until we know more, don't fret.'

'I'll do plenty of that.' She frowned. 'And I'm sorry I was rude. I know you're a good man who—'

Gunshots tore out. Forks clattered as customers dropped them to their plates, then looked around, and Cassidy noted that everyone was looking through the window at the bank. Outside raised voices sounded.

'I wish you luck with your search, ma'am,' Cassidy said, getting to his feet. He patted his holster. 'But this is where you and I part company.'

Standing on the corner of the road Jeff Steed watched Blake Kelly's raiders hurtle out of the bank, trying with his open mouth and jerky movements to look as surprised as everyone else was.

Even if he wasn't shocked, he was surprised that he had kept lookout for Blake. Previously, no matter how hungry he had been, he hadn't broken the law, but he figured he didn't owe Carmon's townsfolk any favours. Whether he stood on the corner or not, the raid would still happen. All that would change was the ten dollars in his pocket.

With a barrage of skyward gunshots and much shouting the raiders secured the safe on the back of a wagon. Then they leapt on their horses and galloped away.

Blake didn't come near Jeff so he wouldn't receive the second ten-dollar payment, but he'd known that.

While the townsfolk stared in shocked silence at the receding riders, Jeff rubbed his hands with glee after earning the easiest money that had ever come his way. Then he headed off down the boardwalk to Maude Tyler's Eatery. While he'd been watching for trouble, half his mind had been planning what he'd do after the raid and now he was intent on a mission to buy himself the largest beef steak he'd ever seen.

Unfortunately when he reached the establishment the hubbub was drawing customers outside, making Jeff grind his teeth in frustration as the possibility of eating quickly receded. He started to push through the crowd, then stopped.

One man was standing in clear space. He was precisely the sort of man Blake hadn't expected to be in town and precisely the sort of man Jeff had been paid to look out for. A star gleamed on this man's chest and with efficient orders he was organizing a posse to chase after Blake.

Jeff hated not completing a job, but as Blake had now left town, he reckoned this discovery was none of his business. So with his back to the wall he wormed his way past the men gathering around the lawman, aiming to get his steak ordered while everyone was preoccupied.

Then a vision of the second ten-dollar payment tapped at his thoughts.

He looked at the open eatery door and the enticing smell of burnt fat drifted out to water his mouth, but a sense of duty, albeit somewhat twisted in the circumstances, made him turn away.

Two minutes later he was riding out of Carmon ahead of the eager bustle from the gathering posse.

CHAPTER 2

'Yates ain't ever giving up,' Walker Hobbs said, eyeing the cloud of dust on the horizon. 'We need to move on.'

'I've had enough of running,' Blake Kelly muttered, his face haggard and drawn. 'We need a place to hole up and make a stand.'

Jeff watched this exchange while his tired horse gulped down water from the river. The horses leading the wagon were even more exhausted, white-slicked and panting, and everyone sat stooped in their saddles, looking in just as bad a way.

Blake's keen eyes searched the plains on either side of the river. Shimmering through the heat-haze, perhaps ten miles away, stood a twin-humped ridge, emerging from the plains like a carelessly dumped saddle.

Jeff reckoned they might be able to find a place to hide there, but in his exhausted state the ridge felt as if it were a hundred miles away.

He sighed and hunched forward. The last two days

had been tough.

When Jeff had found Blake, he had been in good spirits as his raiders counted up a haul that had filled two sacks with bills and a third sack with other valuables. Jeff had ensured that his delight had been short-lived and worse, when Sheriff Cassidy Yates and the posse had ridden into view even more quickly than he had expected, he'd had to escape with Blake.

As he'd galloped away he had hoped to take the first opportunity that came his way to leave the raiders, but with a relentless posse on their tail, Jeff had had no choice but to flee with them. And for two long days they'd kept on fleeing.

Now, even if his role in the bank raid had been a minor one, Jeff reckoned in the eyes of the law he was now effectively one of the raiders.

After resting for two precious minutes they rode on beside the river. The approaching dust cloud was now speckled as the posse became visible, but Jeff reckoned they still had a ten-minute lead on them and with a destination decided he judged that everyone rode along with renewed hope.

Thirty minutes later they reached the ridge. The river veered around it and to traverse the ridge, they would need to skirt along the edge while avoiding a precipitous drop down to the river below.

'Even if we tried,' Walker said, 'we'd never get the wagon over the ridge.'

'Then we have no choice but to make a stand,' Blake said. With swift gestures, he sent two men off to find somewhere to hole up.

Jim looked at the ridge then at the wagon carrying their haul. An idea tapped at his mind. With everyone waiting for the men to return, he nudged his horse forward to draw alongside Blake.

'Maybe we do have a choice,' he said. 'If we can't get the wagon over the ridge, maybe we should fail in the attempt.'

He went on to outline his plan.

'That's a long-shot,' Blake said, his eyes narrowing with scepticism.

'I know, but I'd sooner try something instead of being cornered by Yates's posse. And if it fails, we can still make a stand.'

Blake pondered and slowly a smile appeared. 'For a man I hired for twenty dollars, you sure are worth every cent. If we ever get out of this, you'll get an equal share of the haul.'

Two days ago Jeff would have sooner died than accept such an offer, but he figured he was now in too deep to reject it. He grunted an acceptance and was pleased to hear most of the raiders murmur that they agreed with his plan and with Blake's offer. Blake then considered his men, his furtive glances conveying that he was weighing up who he could trust the most.

As Jeff had expected, he drew Walker aside and spoke with him. Apparently Walker had been with him since the start and if anyone could be relied upon not to take advantage of the situation, it'd be him.

Five minutes later the first man returned and his

report that there was nowhere to hole up close to the river made everyone fidget, wondering if they'd have to make a stand in the open, after all. But to everyone's relief the second man Tex Stroud returned and reported that he'd found a dried-out rill that was wide enough for a few men to hole up in, although not everyone.

'Then that decides it,' Blake said. 'Walker, take two men with you.'

Jeff didn't know if he should be pleased when the first man Walker pointed at was him and then with time pressing he indicated Tex.

'See you at Hard Canyon, Blake,' Walker said.

Blake nodded. Since fleeing Carmon the nearest they'd come to escaping was when for several hours they'd hidden in a cave at Hard Canyon, but after Yates had smoked them out, he shouldn't expect them to return.

With each man taking a sack bulging with the stolen haul, Tex led Jeff and Walker to the rill. Following on behind two men batted away their hoofprints.

The thin rill was deep and with it veering to the side to avoid a boulder at the entrance, Jeff judged that a rider could pass by without noticing it even if he were only a few dozen yards away.

Once inside, Walker ordered Tex to take up a lookout position on one side while he and Jeff took the other side. Keeping low Jeff watched the raiders climb up the ridge. While the wagon brought up the rear, several riders hurried on ahead to make it hard for Yates to work out that some of them had gone missing.

Five minutes later the posse came into view.

He counted thirty men, about the same number that had been preparing to leave Carmon, proving they were still as determined as ever. Sheriff Yates was riding up front urging everyone on and for not the first time Jeff wished that when he'd first seen him he'd just walked into the eatery and filled himself with steak until he burst.

To his relief the posse followed Blake. Then all he could do was watch in pensive silence as the two groups of riders clambered up the ridge. He found that he wasn't the only one to be nervous when Walker joined him.

'Not knowing is about as bad as being chased,' Walker said, his gaze rising to take in the distant receding figures.

Jeff wiped sweat from his brow. 'But less tiring.'

Walker started to smile then froze and pointed. Jeff narrowed his eyes and although he was too far away to discern all the details, he saw that Blake was now carrying out his plan.

The wagon became unhitched and rolled down the slope towards the river, the apparent accident being closely followed by faint cries of alarm. With much shouting and gesticulating at each other, several raiders moved to reclaim the wagon that was speeding away from them. But when it trundled out of Jeff's view getting faster in its descent towards the river they gave up the hopeless rescue attempt and fled.

Two minutes later the posse arrived at the point where the wagon had come loose. Jeff crossed his fingers as this was the moment when Cassidy had to decide whether catching Blake or reclaiming the stolen money was most important. As it turned out he chose the third option of splitting up with most of the posse following the wagon down to the river and around ten men following Blake.

Jeff judged this an acceptable result as unencumbered by the wagon Blake had a chance to get away. Later, when the remainder of the posse found nothing on the wagon, even if they could reach it in the water, they might presume the money had been lost. At best this could dishearten them into giving up and at the least sow further confusion.

Both men watched until everyone had disappeared from view. Then Walker turned to him.

'Hot damn!' he said, punching the air with delight. 'It worked.'

'It sure did,' Jeff said. 'How long do we wait?'

'If after three hours we've seen nobody, we move on.' Rattling sounded. Then Walker placed a coiled loop of a gun and gunbelt on the ground beside Jeff. 'Take it. You're one of us now.'

Walker slapped Jeff's back and then with his head down he edged along the top of the rill to resume keeping lookout.

Jeff eyed the gun, noting that since he'd approached Blake in Carmon he'd taken one step at a time and each one had been a bad step. Taking the weapon was another bad move, but he figured he had no choice. If his plan failed, he'd have to defend himself.

He strapped on the gun then watched the ridge. Every moment he expected Sheriff Yates to ride into view and level a formidable array of guns on them. But Yates didn't show and neither did anyone else. He decided that seeing nothing was good news, but with only guesswork available he had to judge how much time had passed and so the hours dragged.

The sun had swung round and lowered by some distance when impatience got the better of him and he slipped back from his position. The horses and sacks of valuables were below, but he couldn't see either of his associates.

Bemused now, he shuffled along the edge of the rill with his head down. He moved quietly and so when Walker came into view lying on his front with a rifle at his side and his hat pulled down low he didn't alert him.

'Walker,' he whispered in an urgent tone as he approached, 'seen anything yet?'

Walker didn't react, making Jeff smile, judging that he had slipped off to sleep. So he crept up on him, hoping to catch him unawares and so raise a laugh out of his sloth.

Then he saw the wet patch around his head, shining dark red in the light from the lowering sun.

Jeff hurried to Walker's side and rolled him over. Walker's head rocked back to thud against the solid rock with a boneless motion that no living person should have, revealing a sliced throat.

Jeff recoiled then stood in shocked silence running his gaze over the scene and confirming that he hadn't been mistaken. Then he drew his gun and hurried down into the rill to alert Tex, but when he reached the bottom he couldn't see him, although he saw spots of blood dotted about.

Jeff had expected that an assault from Sheriff Yates, if it came, would be a direct one that took advantage of his superior numbers, not a sneak attack like this. Cautiously Jeff approached his horse while looking around the rill.

Behind him a footfall sounded.

Jeff's heightened senses let him react instantly. He swung round, his gun picking out the man sneaking up on him from behind. The man froze, his knife held high and catching a glint from the low sun, temporarily dazzling Jeff. But when he'd blinked away his shock he had a second surprise.

The man was Tex, bloodied knife thrust high, aiming to slash it round at his throat, only Jeff's drawn gun halting him.

'Seems we've got ourselves a situation,' Tex said, smirking.

'We ain't,' Jeff said, now understanding what had happened here. 'You move that knife one inch closer and I'll blast you to hell.'

Tex shrugged. 'I reckon I can stick you before you tighten that trigger finger, but if I can't, the gunshot will echo all round this ridge. Do you want to tell Sheriff Yates where you are?'

Jeff ignored the taunt, although his frown probably conveyed that he didn't want to risk making a noise if he could avoid it.

'Why did you do it, Tex?' he asked.

'A twelfth wasn't enough.'

Jeff shook his head. 'I was happy with twenty dollars so a twelfth was more than enough for me.'

Tex glanced at his knife then at Jeff's gun, appraising their stand-off.

'So if you were happy with a twelfth,' he said, offering a beaming smile, 'what do you say to a half?'

CHAPTER 3

'What happened while I was away?' Sheriff Cassidy Yates asked as he walked into Monotony's law office.

Deputy Floyd Wright looked up from his desk. His firm jaw and narrowed eyes showed he was considering whether to ask the obvious question.

'So you didn't catch him, then?' he said finally, while offering a sympathetic wince.

'Nope,' Cassidy said, sitting on the edge of Wright's desk and summing up three weeks of frustration in one word.

After Blake Kelly's wagon had rolled into the river, he'd searched for the money, but found nothing. In the confusion Blake had escaped and he'd not seen him again. Later Marshal McCoy had taken control of the posse, but after three weeks of fruitless searching in which one by one most of the posse had left he'd also had to admit he was wasting his time.

'Get close?'

'Perhaps. McCoy reckoned they'd split us and we

were herding some of them towards Monotony, but. . . .'

Cassidy shrugged and wisely Wright didn't press for more details. Instead he turned his attention to Cassidy's original question and nodded towards the row of cells at the back of the office where several drunks were snoring like rasping saws.

'We just had the usual fights in the Golden Star.' Wright raised his eyebrows then pointed at the endmost cell. 'But you'll be interested in a man I brought in last night.'

In his irritated state Cassidy snorted at the unlikely possibility of this turning out to be the case then headed over to the cell. Inside a young man was lying on his cot, an arm held over his face. Unlike the other prisoners he wasn't snoring.

'What did he do?' Cassidy asked. His question made the prisoner raise his arm and look at him with bleary eyes. Cassidy didn't recognize him.

'Got too drunk and too ornery, but not so drunk that he couldn't give a name – Samuel Holmes.'

The name meant nothing to Cassidy, but with Wright saying nothing else, he looked again at the young man and this time his high forehead and sparse fair whiskers were slightly familiar.

'The son of Frank Holmes from the Bleak Point silver mine?' Cassidy watched Wright nod then raised his voice to get the prisoner's attention. 'So what's your story, Samuel?'

Samuel sat up on his cot then gingerly placed his feet on the floor with the air of a man who feared he might break a limb if he moved too quickly. He held his head in his hands, rolled his shoulders, then got to his feet slowly and faced Cassidy with his eyes half-closed.

'Can't it wait?' he murmured, then paused to gulp. 'A herd of longhorns are rampaging around my head and the room just won't keep still.'

Samuel flopped down on his cot, uttered a self-pitying sigh, then resumed his posture of lying down while holding his arm over his face.

'I see you regret your behaviour last night,' Cassidy said, 'but I ain't got the time to waste. Talk.'

He waited but didn't get an answer then turned to Wright, who looked aloft, sighing.

'As you can see,' Wright said, 'Samuel ain't half the man his father is. Do you know Patrick Carey?'

'Haven't met him, but I know he took over at the supply depot last month. What's he got to do with this one?'

'Since the snow melted the miners have been waiting for their first supplies of the year, but they didn't arrive. With life getting mighty tough Frank sent out young Samuel to find out why there'd been a delay. The trouble is, in Raw Creek he found out that Patrick had sent those supplies, but they never made it across the Barren Plains.'

'I'm sure the miners can afford to order a new set of supplies.'

'Which is half the problem. Samuel needs to re-order, but their urgent need wasn't quite so urgent that he couldn't find the time to try to drink the saloon dry last night. So the longer he lies in there moaning, the longer the miners will go hungry.'

'Understood.' Cassidy rattled the bars. 'Samuel, you're free to go, but that's only because I know your father. So take this as a warning and don't cause no problems here again.'

'I feel sick,' Samuel murmured, still not raising his arm. 'I ain't going nowhere.'

'I hate to think how hungry your father is right now.' Cassidy waited for Samuel to show some backbone and get up, but he continued to grumble, so he drew Wright away from the cell. 'There are plenty of saloons in town, so we can't rely on this worthless varmint to order those supplies quickly. Perhaps we should get the order in ourselves.'

'I hoped you'd say that, and I also hoped you might be interested enough to find out why the supplies didn't get through.'

'I'm worried about how the miners are faring, but Bleak Point is out of my territory and a tough journey, especially across the Barren Plains.'

'You might change your mind when you see what Samuel picked up in Raw Creek.' Wright withdrew a Wanted poster from his pocket and turned it round for Cassidy to see. 'The supplies were raided by a bandit gang that is being called the Dark Riders. This man is their leader.'

Cassidy considered the grim portrayal then tore the poster from Wright's grasp.

Ten minutes later he was riding out of Monotony with the grumbling and green-tinged Samuel

Holmes in tow, his destination: Patrick Carey's supply depot.

'We must have thrown them off our trail this time,' Jeff Steed said.

'Don't count on it,' Tex said. 'We've thought that twice already.'

Jeff leaned forward in his seat to look down the rail tracks at the depot then took a deep breath and offered the suggestion that had been on his mind for the last few days.

'We have to leave the money somewhere and come back for it later.'

Tex turned in the saddle and opened his mouth to offer what looked as if it'd be a strident refusal then closed it and rubbed his jaw, the thought that had concerned Jeff probably coming to him.

Both men still spent as much time watching the other for signs of treachery as they spent looking out for their pursuers. If they hid the sacks then escaped, one way or the other, both men knew only one of them would return to reclaim them.

'Maybe we should bury the money,' Tex said finally. He pointed at a rise a quarter-mile from the rail tracks. 'We'll find somewhere quiet.'

'All right,' Jeff said, looking at the depot, which from 200 yards away appeared deserted. 'But let's check out this place first.'

'We can't. We need to avoid people.'

'And what better place to do it than here?'

Tex looked at the depot and on noting its quietness he gave a reluctant nod. So they headed along the tracks. Tex continued to grumble, but Jeff couldn't blame him.

Since they'd double-crossed Blake Kelly, they'd not seen him, but they guessed he'd either escaped or been dealt with because the relentless posse were certainly after them. Everywhere, eagle-eyed men were on the lookout and after travelling in circles they were still only fifty miles away from Carmon. They were now trapped near the town of Monotony and every direction they tried was blocked as their pursuers herded them into a smaller and smaller area.

Tex looked haunted and although Jeff had exchanged his tattered clothing for Walker's, he guessed he also looked as guilty as he felt, making it impossible for them to blend in anywhere.

Accordingly both men acted cautiously when Jeff pulled up the wagon beside a door on the side of the first building, a huge wooden construction with wide double-doors facing the railroad tracks. A painted sign above the door identified the buildings as being Patrick Carey's Supplies. After a quick consultation they headed for the door and peered inside.

The interior was cool, dark and quiet. Jeff couldn't tell if it was unoccupied as so much produce had been stored. Bags, crates, sacks were stacked fifteen-feet high in dozens of rows around the sides with only the central aisle being uncluttered.

The two men paced into that area and looked around. Jeff now saw that they were the only people inside and so he headed to an area that interested him. Here, the stored sacks resembled the sacks that contained their money.

'I know what you're thinking,' Tex said, shaking his head, 'and it's a bad idea. If we hide the money here, when we come back, it could be a thousand miles away with no way to find it.'

'Then perhaps we should find out when the next train is due,' Jeff mused.

Tex paced along beside the row of sacks. He kicked several and grunted then made his slow way back to Jeff.

'No,' he said. 'Somebody could still—'

'Hey!' a strident voice barked out. 'What are you two doing?'

Both men turned to see a man pace through the double doors.

'We weren't doing nothing,' Tex bleated, his high-pitched and shocked tone implying the opposite.

'I've been in this business for twenty years and seen all manner of varmints trying to steal whatever they can lay their hands on.' The man snorted a laugh as he continued to walk towards them. 'You'd be the first ones who were doing nothing.'

'It's not like that,' Jeff said, his mind working quickly to conjure up a tale that wouldn't make this man even more suspicious than he was already. 'You'd be Patrick Carey?'

'I am,' he said, stomping to a halt. He looked them up and down, taking in their trail-dirty clothing and fevered eyes with scepticism.

'In that case, you're the man we came to see. We have goods to sell and we were looking for somewhere to store them, for a small fee of course.'

Jeff reached into his pocket and treated Patrick to a flash of a wad of bills, removing some of the scepticism from his eyes.

'How small?' he asked, moving forward.

'If you could give us space for a hundred sacks, ten dollars a month would be fair.'

Jeff didn't know if that was a reasonable offer, but he hoped that the mention of such a large amount of produce to store would placate Patrick and let them leave without further questioning.

'It'd be fair for you, but a hundred sacks takes up a lot of space.'

'It does. So perhaps this isn't the right place to take our custom.' Jeff edged back a pace, preparing to leave. 'We're sure to need even more space later when everything becomes available.'

'More?' Patrick pondered. 'What are you selling?'

Jeff had hoped he wouldn't ask that question.

'I'm glad you asked that,' he said. Stalling for time, he turned to look along the rows of sacks and crates, searching for an idea that would sound plausible, but no thoughts would come.

'But what is it?' Patrick persisted advancing on him. 'Because I'm not interested in any dubious scheme. I run a—'

Patrick screeched, the sound quickly cutting off.

Jeff swirled round to see that Tex had stepped up behind Patrick and had clamped a hand over his mouth. Tex's shoulders were bunched and his eyes were gleaming, while Patrick's chest arched forward and his eyes were pained.

Tex smirked and jerked backwards, releasing his hold of Patrick. The storeman fell to the ground to lie on his chest, displaying the knife protruding from his back.

'You didn't need to do that,' Jeff said.

'Sure did,' Tex said, bending down to rip out the knife with a flourish. He wiped it on Patrick's shirt before slipping it back in his belt. 'You weren't talking us out of this and we can't take no chances.'

'Except you've just condemned us. Nobody would care about Walker's murder, but this man's death is a different matter.'

'Quit complaining and help me move the body. We need to bury him somewhere where nobody will ever find him, same as the money.'

Jeff took Patrick's legs and helped Tex carry the body to the door while shaking his head in annoyance now that what had seemed a promising idea to get them out of trouble had got them into even worse trouble.

When he nudged the door open with his back, he looked over his shoulder then stopped. Two riders were approaching along the railroad tracks.

'Get back in,' he urged.

'Too late,' Tex muttered. 'They've seen us.'

'But perhaps not the body.'

Tex glanced at his knife. 'If you're wrong, we'll be digging holes for two more bodies.'

'We won't,' Jeff said, determined to avoid the death-toll from their ill-advised partnership rising even higher. 'I'll find us another way out of this.'

'Come on, Samuel,' Cassidy said to his disgruntled companion. 'The quicker we get there, the quicker we can order those goods.'

Samuel plucked up enough enthusiasm to sneer, although it had no effect on Cassidy as he'd already decided that sneering was his only response to any request. Despite Cassidy's stern expression, Samuel pointed back along the railroad tracks.

'Why couldn't I stay in Monotony? I've got an awful thirst on now.'

'I brought you because every minute we waste is another minute your father and the rest of the miners have to spend hungry.'

'If they're that hungry, they can always leave.'

Cassidy sighed. After spending two hours with Samuel, he was no nearer to understanding him. Frank Holmes was an old friend whom he hadn't seen for some years, but so far the only thing he'd gathered about Samuel was that he was nothing like his father.

'They mine silver. They'll never leave that.'

'You can't eat silver. You can't drink silver. And silver sure ain't good company, if you know what I mean.'

The leer Samuel provided left Cassidy in no doubt what he meant. As to reach Bleak Point they'd have to pass through Carmon and Raw Creek, he could see he would face plenty of problems ensuring Samuel didn't seek out entertainment on the way.

'You can forget about that. We have a mission to complete.'

With that comment Cassidy gave Samuel a long warning glare then turned to the depot. It appeared deserted, but he guessed it probably always looked like that when a train wasn't in and he was sure he'd seen a door open and close earlier. He dismounted beside that door and tethered his horse behind a wagon containing three sacks.

With Samuel tagging along behind he wandered around the building, calling out for Patrick Carey. Nobody emerged and neither did anyone appear when he called out beside the other two buildings.

He stood, listening, but could hear only the wind whistling through the buildings and the steady drip from a leaking pump beside the rail tracks.

'All this way for nothing,' Samuel grumbled. 'I told you we should have stayed in town.'

'You'd better hope it's not for nothing, because we're not leaving until we've found Patrick.'

Samuel muttered to himself, but Cassidy's gloomy forecast proved hasty when a man emerged from around the side of the final building. Another man lurked behind him, but he stayed at the corner of the building and eyed them with surly contempt. Both men were rough-clad, sweat-slicked and stooped, presumably from hard work.

'What you want?' the nearest man asked as he approached.

'I want so see Patrick Carey,' Cassidy said.

The man started to reply but then his gaze fell on Cassidy's star and stuck there. He stopped walking and looked up to consider him. His eyes narrowed with recognition before he looked over his shoulder at the second man. Cassidy reckoned a silent message passed before the man turned back.

'You a friend of his?'

'Never met him, but my business is urgent.'

For long moments the man considered him while the second man slipped backwards until he loitered at the corner of the building.

'I'm Patrick Carey,' the man declared finally, his voice breaking with an odd change of tone.

'Then I'm afraid I have bad news for you. You sent out a shipment of supplies to the silver miners at Bleak Point?' Cassidy had phrased his comment as a question, but Patrick didn't respond. 'It never arrived.'

Patrick rocked from foot to foot then shrugged.

'No refunds.'

'I'm sure the miners are less concerned about a refund than getting a replacement shipment, and you should be less concerned about a refund than what's happened to your workers.'

Patrick winced. 'They can take care of themselves.'

'I hope they can, but I intend to head out to Bleak Point to see if I can find out what happened to the shipment. If you could get together a replacement set of supplies, I can ride with them.'

'We ain't exactly. . . .' Patrick frowned, glanced

back at the other man, then raised a hand. 'Wait here. I have to talk about this.'

He headed off to join the other man and they disappeared from view around the corner of the building. A conversation took place. From thirty yards away Cassidy couldn't hear what was said, but he did hear their low and urgent tones.

Patrick's odd reaction had bemused him, but then again after riding with Samuel he'd become used to people behaving in an odd manner. Presently, Patrick returned on his own.

'Have you got a list?' he asked.

Cassidy gestured to Samuel who presented Patrick with two pages of scrawled details.

'That's our previous order,' Samuel said.

Patrick considered the list, rubbing his jaw, then nodded.

'There's plenty here, but we should have it ready within two hours.'

'That's good news.' Cassidy looked around. 'Can you round up enough people to take it out to Bleak Point?'

'Nope. There's just me and . . . me and Mike, but we're all you need.' Patrick smiled. 'We'll deliver the supplies ourselves.'

'I sure hope this is labelled up right,' Jeff said, swinging the sack up on to his shoulder.

'Who cares?' Tex said, glaring at the next item on what seemed to be an endless list. 'We ain't going all the way to Bleak Point.'

'I guess not.' Jeff snorted a laugh. He'd become so absorbed with finding the required produce he'd temporarily forgotten they were engaged in a ruse to escape from the closing posse.

Luckily when they'd been with Blake, Sheriff Yates hadn't got close enough to see their features and, as he'd not asked any tricky questions, they assumed he believed they were who they said they were. But as coming across the body of Patrick Carey would have destroyed that belief, Jeff had tasked Cassidy and his idle companion with getting three wagons ready to leave.

Tex had then taken the body away and buried it in a secluded place beyond the rise while Jeff had bumbled along locating the goods. But on his return Tex was still sceptical.

'And I don't see this working, Jeff,' Tex said, for what Jeff reckoned was the fifth time.

Jeff had doubts himself, but to escape from the net that was inexorably closing on them, they just needed some luck and to maintain their disguises for a while. Then, when they'd thrown off their pursuers and before Tex killed again, they hoped a convenient excuse would present itself that would let them leave Cassidy.

Jeff had explained all this before so he tried a different approach.

'Marshal McCoy is in charge of the posse now and he's looking for bank raiders. He's not looking for a convoy of supplies and especially not for one being escorted by the very sheriff who was chasing after us in the first place!' Jeff waited until Tex started to disagree then spoke over him. 'And whether you accept that or not, you will call me Patrick, Mike.'

Tex considered for a moment then smirked and reached over to pat his back.

'All right, Patrick. I'll go along with your plan.' He chuckled. 'And if it works, it'll sure be a kick in the teeth for both lawmen.'

Jeff nodded then turned to the door. While still chortling Tex swung a sack of corn onto his shoulder and followed.

Outside, Cassidy was hitching up the last two horses. Samuel was sitting on a fence, chewing on a piece of grass and staring vacantly into space, as he had done since they'd begun work.

They dumped the sacks on the back of the third wagon and stood back, counting. Jeff avoided looking at the first wagon where beneath several crates they'd hidden the sacks containing the proceeds of the bank raid.

'Everything loaded?' Cassidy asked.

Jeff compared their tally to the list. They'd loaded three-quarters of what the miners had requested. But with Cassidy having completed his task, he didn't want to draw attention to their fumbling search for the remaining items. So he considered the wagons and decided they had already loaded enough produce to present a realistically sized convoy.

'Yeah,' he said. 'We're ready to move on out.'

Cassidy appraised the heaped piles of produce.

'Do we have enough people to do this?'

'Three wagons, four people . . . should be enough.'

'It'll be tiring work.' Cassidy pointed at Samuel. 'And that useless waste of skin won't be much use. But we'll pass through Carmon, so I guess we can get help there if we need it.'

Jeff didn't intend to stop anywhere where they could be recognized, or more likely be recognized as not being who they said they were, but to avoid delaying their departure with an unnecessary discussion, he nodded.

Only then did Samuel wander over. He looked at the convoy then reported he'd ride his horse and let them take care of the wagons. When Cassidy swung round to glare at him, Jeff moved back to let them resolve that brewing argument while he decided which wagon he'd prefer to drive.

If he stayed with the lead wagon, he could keep close to the sacks containing the haul. On the other hand if Tex drove it, he could keep an eye on him and look out for signs of deception.

As it turned out Tex took the decision from him when he climbed up on the lead wagon without comment. Jeff noted that he'd done that then chose the middle wagon, leaving the irritated Cassidy to take the final one.

'With this size of convoy it'll be Carmon by mid-afternoon tomorrow,' Jeff said to Cassidy, using information he'd gleaned from the map he'd found in Patrick's office. 'Raw Creek after another five days, and then it's six days across the Barren Plains to Bleak Point.'

Cassidy nodded. 'I hope to beat that schedule as I'll have plenty of scouting around to do to find out what happened to the previous convoy.'

Jeff swung up onto the seat. Although he'd decided not to overdo his apparent concern, he asked the question he thought Patrick would have asked.

'Do you know what happened to it?'

Cassidy jumped up onto the seat of the final wagon.

'I hope nothing,' he called out, 'but the rumour in Raw Creek was that a bandit gang has taken refuge out in the Barren Plains. Some think they raided the convoy.'

Jeff nodded, but then the full ramifications of what Cassidy had said hit him.

'Which bandits?' he asked with mounting trepidation.

'They've become known as the Dark Riders and are led by Blake Kelly.' Cassidy glanced at his gun. 'And I have a score to settle with him.'

CHAPTER 4

'Keep looking straight ahead,' Jeff murmured to himself, while willing Tex to do the same.

The meeting he wanted to avoid – or as he now knew the first of the difficult meetings – was imminent. Marshal McCoy was ahead. Waiting on the trail with him were five riders.

Jeff narrowed his eyes looking for signs of trouble, although what he'd do if he saw them he didn't know. They were riding into a situation from which even Tex's murderous appetites couldn't extricate them.

He was surprised by how few men McCoy had with him, as he'd appeared to have many more when the posse had been closing in on them. But now that he was in a more confident frame of mind, he wondered if he had been mistaken. Perhaps his guilty conscience had made it appear that everyone who had looked at them did so suspiciously.

Either way, he'd find out soon enough whether his plan would get them through McCoy's net.

As the lead wagon approached McCoy, the riders stayed put, making sure the convoy stopped. Jeff hoped Tex would stop as even if the marshal didn't recognize them, riding on would raise his suspicions, but Tex carried on at the same speed. Either the riders would move aside or he'd run them down.

Jeff was wondering whether he should shout at Tex to pull up when Cassidy called out from behind.

'Howdy, Marshal McCoy,' he shouted, standing in his seat and waving. 'It's Cassidy. Move aside.'

Jeff breathed a sigh of relief when the riders parted and McCoy moved towards Cassidy. Tex shook the reins hurrying the wagons on through the gap in the riders while keeping his gaze set forward. Trying not to draw attention on himself as he passed through, Jeff hunched down on the seat and looked straight ahead.

He heard Cassidy pulling up behind him and, from the corner of his eye, he saw McCoy ride by, but the marshal didn't give him so much as a second glance. He couldn't help but smile as again his plans appeared to have fooled a lawman.

Then he concentrated on enjoying the sight of the open trail ahead, something he never thought he'd see again.

'Onward to Bleak Point,' he said to himself, as he let himself imagine that he wasn't a fleeing bank raider. Instead he was doing what he'd wanted to do when he'd first ridden into Carmon: he was just an ordinary man doing an ordinary job.

Perhaps that was no longer an impossible dream.

*

'You're wrong,' Marshal McCoy said. 'Blake Kelly hasn't had the time to reach the Barren Plains and to start raiding convoys. We've definitely fenced him in around Monotony.'

'Maybe he has and maybe he hasn't,' Cassidy said. 'All I know is a convoy of supplies has gone missing beyond Raw Creek and the rumour is that Blake was responsible.'

McCoy looked at Cassidy for long moments before he replied.

'We both know how rumours start. People hear about a bank raid and before long every time somebody stubs a toe Blake's responsible.' McCoy waited until Cassidy gave a rueful nod then pointed at the other two wagons, which were now 200 yards on and kicking up plumes of dust as they trundled away at high speed. 'But they're sure in a hurry to find out the truth.'

'Can't blame them. Patrick's workers were with the missing convoy.'

McCoy nodded. 'Then I'll leave you to your mission, and good luck to whichever one of us finds him.'

Cassidy considered the men with McCoy, noting their diminished numbers, but he decided that if he didn't ask he wouldn't find out.

'Before you go,' he said, 'can you spare anyone?'

'Sorry, Cassidy. Everyone is tired. Only the feeling we're getting close is keeping us going. A journey to

Bleak Point is too much to ask.'

Cassidy nodded and after bidding McCoy good fortune he moved his wagon off after the receding Patrick and Mike and returned his thoughts to the problem that had worried him before. He understood why his new companions were determined not to waste time, but he didn't understand why Patrick didn't want to hire more help on the way.

His conversation with McCoy had focused his mind on the fact that putting aside the hard work, if he were to come up against Blake he'd need help. So he hoped Patrick would have changed his mind by the time they arrived in Carmon as it'd save him the trouble of having to change it for him.

As he gained on the second wagon, Patrick glanced back and, on seeing that Cassidy had left McCoy, he hollered something to Mike who also glanced back. Then both men set their gazes forward and first one man then the other bunched a fist and shook it, perhaps in a gesture of triumph.

That observation following on from their frequently sneaky behaviour sent Cassidy's mind racing. Within moments a clear idea formed – they were hiding something.

As soon as he'd considered this, many minor odd incidents throughout the last day fitted into place. Previously he'd put their shifty glances and furtive postures down to tiredness, the natural suspicion most people had when they had goods to protect, and worry about what had happened to the previous convoy. But people with an ulterior motive also acted in that way.

There were many possibilities: Patrick was over-charging the miners; the previous convoy had been a cover for trafficking something other than food; the convoy hadn't even gone to Bleak Point in the first place. Cassidy hoped it wasn't the latter, but after deciding there was something odd going on, he was even more determined to stop at Carmon and hire men.

As it was, when they pulled up on the edge of town and Cassidy stated his opinion Patrick wrong-footed him.

'I agree,' he said without complaint. 'I've been thinking and a journey to Bleak Point through the bandit-infested Barren Plains is risky. We need at least another eight men.'

'Glad you're now thinking that way,' Cassidy said, 'and don't worry about the cost. I have funds to cover hiring men on this type of mission.'

'Obliged for the offer, but these men won't be deputies. They'll work for me, so I'll pay them, but if the situation calls for it I'll let them help you.' Patrick waited until Cassidy accepted these terms. 'And that means we'll head into town to do the hiring while you look after the wagons.'

Cassidy was minded to disagree with this last demand, but he guessed that Patrick would dig in his heels on matters that encroached on his command of the convoy, so he nodded.

With that matter settled Mike joined Patrick to head off while for the first time that day Samuel showed some interest in what was happening. He stood beside Cassidy and peered into town longingly.

'If they're leaving to do some hiring,' he said, 'and you're looking after the wagons, can I go into town?'

Cassidy sighed with exasperation. He was minded to bark out a demand that he help for the first time. Then he thought about the long journey ahead and about Samuel's previous comments about looking for entertainment. The only town between here and Bleak Point was Raw Creek and that wasn't a fit place for anyone to venture into alone.

'All right,' he said. 'You can go.'

'But only for one hour,' Patrick said, turning back to waggle a finger with a mock stern warning. 'Then we're leaving, with or without you.'

'Obliged,' Samuel said, grinning. 'But can I have some money? I've only got a dollar and—'

'No, you can't,' Patrick grunted with vehemence, his jovial mood snapping away in an instant. 'A dollar is more than the likes of you deserves when you're not prepared to do even a minute's work.'

Samuel considered Patrick's flared eyes then Mike's surly glare. He gulped, tipped his hat to Cassidy, then slunk off into town.

'You were harsh on him there,' Cassidy said.

'Somebody needs to be,' Patrick said, watching the young man speed to a trot as the lure of the big town drew him on. 'Are you sure about letting him go?'

'Yeah,' Cassidy said. 'I mean, how much trouble can he get into in an hour?'

*

'This is a bad idea,' Tex grumbled as he approached the first saloon on the main road.

'Quit worrying,' Jeff said. 'Nobody saw our faces when we were here before and even if they did, nobody would expect us to walk back into town.'

'I didn't mean coming into town, I meant the hiring part. We don't need anyone. We're not going to Bleak Point, remember?'

Jeff halted and drew Tex round to face him.

'But we have to appear that we are. Marshal McCoy chased us for weeks but when he met us he thought we were looking after the convoy and didn't give us a second glance. The disguise works. Now we just have to leave the convoy before we meet Blake and without making Cassidy suspicious. If we have more men looking after the supplies, it'll be easier to find a reason.'

Tex sneered. 'It'd be easier to slash his throat.'

Jeff winced as Tex mentioned the biggest reason why he wanted to hire men: avoiding the death-toll growing any higher.

'It won't,' Jeff said, choosing a retort that Tex might accept. 'Cassidy's a formidable lawman. You're more likely to get yourself killed.'

Tex looked back at the wagons on the edge of the town then gave a brief nod.

'All right. We hire men and keep up this nonsense until Raw Creek, but no further.' He looked through the saloon window, shaking his head. 'Provided we can find someone for hire who doesn't know Patrick Carey.'

Tex's traditional gloomy forecast made Jeff smile, but thirty minutes and four saloons later he was no longer smiling. In each saloon they had asked about Patrick Carey and everyone had known and had wanted to talk about him. Apparently before he'd taken over at the depot he'd worked in Carmon and nobody had a good word to say about him.

As they walked towards the final saloon on the road, desperation had overcome Jeff's contented mood. Even worse, he'd met Blake in this saloon and he didn't want to risk going somewhere where he might be recognized.

'Perhaps you were right,' he said.

Tex grunted. 'Glad you've finally admitted that. But I've been thinking. Perhaps we're looking in the wrong places.'

He set off for a side road. Jeff was so pleased that Tex was showing an interest in maintaining their cover that he didn't complain, although he was minded to when he saw what he had in mind.

Away from the main road and the brightly lit saloons, like all towns, Carmon had the kind of establishments that were so dingy even Jeff wouldn't have frequented them before his life had taken a major change.

Tex had no such qualms. He headed for a dimly lit ramshackle building on the edge of town. He walked in, appraised the blank-eyed men nursing glasses on their own, then slammed a discarded glass on the bar gathering the attention of the men who weren't asleep or too drunk to respond.

'Who knows Patrick Carey?' he demanded.

Nobody replied, although a few men grunted at him to be quiet.

'Anyone ever met him?' he persisted.

This time a man from down the bar raised his head to sneer.

'I've heard he pays the lowest wages around. Nobody will work for him.'

'Somebody always will,' Tex said, but the man waved in a dismissive manner at him and returned to his drink.

Tex snorted, his hunched shoulders suggesting he was ready to start an argument, but Jeff tapped his arm then drew his attention to a new man who was wending his way towards them. His clothing was as tattered as Jeff's had been three weeks ago and Jeff recognized the despair in his eyes.

'Are you hiring?' the man asked.

'We are, but only. . . .' Jeff pondered, choosing his words carefully. 'Only people who haven't worked for Patrick Carey before.'

'Or met him,' Tex said, bunching a fist with a hint of the treatment he'd mete out to people who failed their requirements.

Jeff winced at the unsubtle comment, but it didn't perturb the man.

'I've never heard of him,' he said. 'Then again I ain't from around these parts, but I just want to say, I'll do anything.'

'Anything, eh?' Jeff smiled and beckoned for the man to join them. 'We're several men short so we have some work for a man who'll do *anything*.'

'Are these men suitable?' Cassidy said, eyeing the motley assortment of men Patrick had clearly rounded up from the roughest saloons in town.

The eight men were grimy and wore tattered clothes. Three men were so drunk they had to be held up and didn't appear to know where they were. Only one man was eyeing the convoy eagerly, but Cassidy reckoned he was wondering what he could steal, and the only completely sober worker was barely a man. His feet were bare and he wore trousers cut off at the knees. His wide-eyed look conveyed that he was a young lad who had run away from home and who had already discovered that life alone wasn't what he'd expected.

'They're ideal,' Patrick said with a glint in his eye that said he knew they were anything but.

'I'd heard you had a reputation for hiring cheap labour, but not this cheap.'

'There ain't much profit in what I do.' Patrick smiled. 'I have to take whatever I can afford.'

Cassidy sighed, deciding he'd struggle to win this argument.

'Do they know about the dangers ahead?'

'They do.' Patrick lowered his voice. 'And to be honest, these were the only ones prepared to face it, but don't worry; men like this are ideal in a tough situation. I'll get them to work and by sundown when we've got some miles under our wheels you'll feel better about them.'

'All right,' Cassidy said, although a glance at the young lad's confused expression that said he didn't know what was expected of him reminded him of another problem. 'But we can't go yet. Samuel's not back.'

Patrick shrugged while Mike looked into town and picked out the clock on the mayor's office.

'We're here for an hour,' Mike grunted. 'He's had fifty minutes. If he's not back in ten minutes, we're leaving – with or without him.'

Cassidy accepted that ultimatum with a curt nod then rolled his shoulders and set off walking purposefully down the road. He heard Patrick and Mike talking behind him then footfalls sounded as Patrick hurried to catch up with him.

'I didn't think,' Cassidy said, 'you were interested in Samuel.'

'I'm not,' Patrick said, 'but I reckon it'd just be easier if we found him in the next ten minutes.'

When they reached town Cassidy considered the numerous saloons on the main road.

'But where to try first?'

Patrick pointed at the third saloon on the road, from where the rattle of breaking furniture and raised voices were sounding.

'You wondered how much trouble he could get into in an hour, so I reckon the place with the most trouble happening is a good place to start.'

Cassidy provided a rueful smile.

'That's a good idea,' he said, as he stepped up on to the boardwalk, 'but surely even he couldn't have got into a fight this quickly.'

'Maybe you're right. He's far too idle to—' A chair crashed through the window, making Patrick duck to avoid it.

Cassidy winced, half-hoping that Patrick was mistaken and half-hoping Samuel was inside so that he didn't have to waste time trying to find him, but he found out soon enough.

When he pushed through the batwings Samuel was facing him at the bar. A burly man was confronting him with an arm thrust out sideways showing he'd hurled the chair away. Samuel was squaring up to him despite the presence of two other men moving in to join his adversary.

Cassidy looked at Patrick, received a nod, then paced across the saloon.

'I'm Sheriff Cassidy Yates,' he said, but as Samuel and his adversary closed on each other a rising clamour of noise from the customers drowned out his words.

So Cassidy paced to the bar and slapped a hand on the shoulder of the man confronting Samuel. He moved to drag him away, but the man jerked his elbow into Cassidy's stomach blasting the air from his chest then threw him backwards against the bar.

Winded, Cassidy could only watch as a brutal swinging punch to the jaw pummelled Samuel to the floor whereupon two men hurried in and grabbed him. One man pinned him down while the other man kicked him then stepped aside for the first man to have his turn. But, as he raised his foot, Patrick thrust his head down and charged him. He hit the man in the side and carried him on for several paces before both men went tumbling to the floor.

The other men stared at Patrick agog, clearly not having expected anyone to step in. Cassidy ensured that Patrick wasn't the only help Samuel would get. While taking deep breaths to free the tightness in his chest he shook himself then paced up to Samuel's other two adversaries.

Behind them, Patrick was tussling with his opponent on the floor, but Cassidy put them from his mind and beckoned the men on. One man stepped ahead of the other and swung back his fist ready to deliver a round-arm punch at Cassidy's face, but he flagged up his motion so clearly that Cassidy easily ducked under the swinging arm. Then he bobbed back up and followed through with a short-arm jab to the man's stomach that made him double over then stagger away coughing.

Then he swung round to the second man who had the presence of mind to take his time. The man circled Cassidy, who was forced to watch him while also watching the first man from the corner of his eye. That man straightened and, not giving him a chance to regain his wits, Cassidy turned on his heel and used his momentum to deliver a haymaker of a punch to his cheek that sent him spinning to the floor. But the circling man took advantage of the distraction and pounding footfalls sounded a moment before he leapt on Cassidy's back.

His weight almost knocked Cassidy to the floor but he managed to stay upright by thrusting out a leg. From behind, the man wrapped a burly arm around his neck making Cassidy gasp for air. Then he clawed at Cassidy's face with his other hand, but by mistake a finger slipped into his mouth. Cassidy bit down hard. He tasted blood and was rewarded when a pained cry sounded and the grip around his neck loosened.

Cassidy didn't give the man a chance to fight back and paced backwards then threw himself at the bar, trapping the man between his back and the wood. Another bleat of pain sounded and so Cassidy rocked forward then threw himself backwards again, and again. On the fourth throw the arm slipped away.

Cassidy swirled round to face the man, who was teetering with his arms thrown out for balance. Cassidy helped him on his way by hurling a fierce uppercut to his chin that knocked him over the bar to land in a crumpled heap on the other side. A glance over the bar confirmed the man was lying prone and groaning before Cassidy turned back to see how Patrick was faring.

He smiled on seeing that Patrick was standing over his pole-axed assailant and even Samuel had gained his feet and was now facing the remaining opponent, who was on his knees preparing to rise, having shaken off Cassidy's last blow.

Cassidy paced towards that man, but when he saw that he was now outnumbered the man raised a hand in submission. Then he shuffled backwards along the floor to lean back against the bar where he rubbed his ribs ruefully and avoided meeting anyone's eye.

Cassidy looked around the saloon to confirm nobody else would take exception to them, and when the customers began to right chairs and return to their previous business he turned to Samuel.

'One hour!' he said. 'How hard was it for you to stay out of trouble for a single hour?'

'It wasn't my fault,' Samuel murmured.

'You said that about all the trouble you caused in Monotony. So whose fault was it this time?'

Cassidy's sarcasm made Samuel curl his upper lip in irritation, although it was hard to tell the difference from his usual sneering expression, but before he could retort a woman spoke up.

'It was mine,' she said from behind Cassidy.

Cassidy swirled round to find he was facing Abigail Scott, the woman he'd abandoned three weeks ago when he'd rounded up the posse to chase Blake Kelly.

'How could this fight be your fault?'

'Because this gallant young man stepped in when I got myself into trouble.' She pointed at the grumbling knocked-down men. 'I tried to hire them, but as it turned out, I'd picked unsuitable men.'

'Why would you want to hire these varmints?'

'Because,' she said, 'I've found out where my sister went.'

CHAPTER 5

'Where did Jane go?' Cassidy asked, as he and Abigail left the saloon with Samuel and Patrick trailing along behind.

'The Barren Plains,' Abigail said.

This revelation made Cassidy come to a sudden halt. As the others bunched up around him he turned to her.

'Mining for silver?'

'That's what I've been told. When she and Ethan came off the train they heard about the silver being dug up there. So they abandoned their plans to set up a home and threw in their lot with two prospectors who had a plan to stake out a new pitch.'

'Abigail, I'm sorry to ask this, but did this story come from a reliable source?'

'I had to pay for it, if that's what you mean.'

'I do. A tale about gullible newcomers to town is believable, but when it's told for money to—'

'Don't say it, Cassidy. I believe what I've been told and I intend to find them whether you help me or not.' She smiled. 'When Samuel stepped in, he told me where you were going.'

Cassidy looked at Samuel aiming to offer an apology, but he'd converted his usual sneer into a smirk so he saved his breath.

'I'll look for them, but you're not coming with us. If they headed to the Barren Plains—'

'I know they were naïve,' she snapped, 'but however dangerous it is out there, I have to go.'

'The Barren Plains being dangerous is only half the problem,' Cassidy said, raising his voice so she couldn't speak over him. 'For every legitimate prospector who's prepared to search there, there's another who claims to be a prospector and who is more interested in getting rich without travelling.'

She had already raised a finger to emphasize her next retort, but then lowered it when she realized what he had meant.

'If they were led out of town then robbed and killed, I'll never find their bodies,' she said, softening her tone. 'So I have to follow this lead.'

Cassidy sighed. The mission was already hard enough with a missing convoy and Blake Kelly's Dark Riders to find while keeping the motley group of workers Patrick had hired in line. But with time pressing he could think of only one way he could stop her continuing to search for someone who'd help her.

'All right,' he said. He gestured at the wagons. 'You can join us, but we're leaving in five minutes. Get ready to go by then or we'll leave without you.'

'That's no way to speak to a lady,' Patrick said, leaning forward and raising his hat to her. 'You take as long as you need, Abigail. We'll wait.'

As Cassidy glared at Patrick, Abigail beamed a huge smile.

'I'll get my buggy,' she said, then turned away.

'You didn't give Samuel that option,' Cassidy said, watching her hurry to the hotel.

'He ain't as pretty as she is,' Patrick said, joining him in watching her.

Cassidy smiled ruefully then as they headed back to the wagons he filed in beside Samuel.

'I guess I owe you an apology,' he said. 'You stepped in to help a woman. That's the sort of—'

'I didn't exactly step in,' Samuel said, licking his lips and leering. 'You wouldn't give me no money and I was looking for company, if you know what I mean. And she looked like the sort of woman who might show me a good time, so I—'

'Don't go no further with that comment,' Patrick snapped.

'Yeah,' Cassidy said, 'and just when I was all set to compliment you for the first time.'

Despite Cassidy's scepticism about the usefulness of the men they'd hired, when they'd sobered up they proved to be hard-working and capable.

Jeff didn't know whether that was because Tex was a better judge of character than he had given him credit for, or because they were trying to appear proficient now that a woman had joined the convoy.

But as the days passed and they trundled away from the scene of their troubles while not encountering any new ones, he grew more relaxed.

Curiously Tex also relaxed and no longer took every moment when they were alone to berate him with his thoughts on how bad a plan this was and how many ways it could fail. Instead, he threw himself into his new role with apparent enthusiasm and this further encouraged Jeff to absorb himself in his assumed role.

In fact, when he took his turn at the reins of the second wagon, for lengthy stretches he forgot he was an on-the-run outlaw who'd double-crossed a bandit. Instead, he imagined that he actually was Patrick Carey leading a convoy sent out by a business he ran.

Although reality ultimately intruded on that fantasy, it did help him to confirm that if he ever got out of this mess, he'd settle down somewhere where nobody knew him and start a business of his own.

As the hired men usually ignored the youngest worker, Todd Lester, when it was Jeff's turn at the reins he took it upon himself to let him ride with him. The attentiveness Todd gave to his snippets of advice and to his made-up tales of his supply-moving exploits, only went to relax him even more.

So Jeff was in a contented frame of mind when they stopped for what would be their last night before they reached Raw Creek. Using the map he'd purloined from the depot he'd chosen a spot beside the creek that gave the town its name, this being the last easy-to-find water they'd have available until they reached Bleak Point.

While everyone milled around and stretched, Todd built then lit a fire between the wagons and the creek. Then while Abigail came over from her buggy to supervise him in preparing a meal and everyone else formed a circle and chatted, Jeff sat alone on a boulder by the water.

He watched Abigail, as he did whenever he was sure she couldn't see him, and wondered whether she was the kind of woman who would be interested in a man like Patrick Carey. He watched her until Cassidy approached him. To cover his discomfort after being caught staring, he looked at the water and pretended to be deep in thought.

'Raw Creek tomorrow?' Cassidy asked.

'Late afternoon, I reckon,' Jeff said, turning to him.

'And then the difficulties start.' Cassidy sat beside him on the boulder. 'I've got plenty of aims and I ain't sure which should take precedence, be it finding the missing convoy, finding Blake Kelly, finding Abigail's sister, or just crossing the Barren Plains and feeding the miners. So I intend to ask around in Raw Creek and see what I can find out. What I hear will decide how we proceed.'

Jeff nodded, choosing his words before he uttered them.

'Remember that I have my priorities too. If I hear anything about the previous convoy, I'm prepared to follow that up with Mike and leave the men I hired to make their own way to Bleak Point.'

Cassidy frowned. 'Splitting up ain't ideal.'

'I know, but that option might make things easier for you if you have conflicting duties.'

'Obliged for the offer,' Cassidy said after thinking it through. He slapped Jeff's shoulder then got up and moved to return to the main group, but then stopped. He stood for a while then turned back. 'Before I go, can I ask you something?'

Jeff got to his feet, sudden dread overcoming the elation he'd felt when Cassidy had accepted his groundwork for leaving.

'Ask away,' he said cautiously.

'What can I do about Samuel?'

Jeff breathed a sigh of relief. Then to cover himself he walked slowly back to the group.

'Nothing,' he said with laughter in his tone. 'He's useless.'

'He is at that.' Cassidy pointed out Todd who was up to his knees in the creek filling a coffee-pot with water. 'Todd is younger than Samuel is, yet he's understood what's expected of him and has thrown himself into every task as if his life depended on it. Samuel wouldn't get out of bed if his life depended on it.'

Jeff nodded. 'Todd hasn't talked about what brought him here, but I reckon he's had a tough life. Samuel hasn't. That's about all the reasoning I can find for his behaviour.'

'Mine too, and I'm sure that's why Frank sent him out. He's sure to face danger and if he can cope, that'll give him some pride in himself. But I don't reckon he'll change. At the first sign of trouble he'll run or do something so stupid he'll get himself killed.'

'The way I see it, it can go two ways, and Frank would have known that when he risked sending him away. He won't blame you if it goes the wrong way.'

'Perhaps he won't, but I will no matter what. . . .' Cassidy trailed off and peered at the wagons with his eyes narrowed.

Jeff followed his gaze to see that on the opposite side of the wagons to the fire, someone was leaning over the side of the lead wagon, his form indistinct in the poor light. Jeff glanced at the main group beside the creek. It didn't take him long to work out who was rummaging.

'It's all right,' he said. 'It's . . . it's Mike.'

'But what's he doing?'

Before Jeff could answer Tex saw them approaching and jerked away from the wagon. While rocking from foot to foot and not meeting their eyes he waited for them to join him. Cassidy repeated his question, but Tex didn't reply and instead cast nervous glances at the wagon, so Jeff spoke up.

'I asked him to check the ropes. We don't want no mishaps when we're passing through a town like Raw Creek.'

'A wise precaution,' Cassidy said. Without any suggestion that he thought anything was amiss he left them to sit beside Abigail, as he did every evening using the excuse that he was making sure none of the workers annoyed her.

Jeff maintained a fixed smile until Cassidy was out of earshot then grabbed Tex's arm and pulled him out of his view.

'Like Cassidy said,' he muttered, 'what were you doing?'

'You know what I was doing,' Tex snapped. 'I'm checking you haven't been sneaking into the sacks and helping yourself to my share.'

'I don't want your share. I'm happy with half. It was more important that nobody suspected we're carrying anything other than supplies. Now that you've acted oddly in front of the lawman, don't do it again, or he'll check in there for himself.'

'Quit telling me what to do.' Tex stabbed a finger at Jeff's chest catching him unawares and rocking him back a pace. 'If he snoops, it'll be the last thing he does.'

Jeff dug in a heel and leaned forward to glare at Tex.

'You are not killing the lawman,' he muttered.

Tex sneered, looking as if he'd continue arguing, then shrugged and raised his hands.

'Stop your whining. Unless the lawman starts prying real soon he'll be safe. I'm not risking meeting Blake in the Barren Plains. We're resting up in Raw Creek tomorrow night. Come the morning, I'll be gone. You can come with me or stay with the convoy, but either way I'm not going no further.'

Jeff sighed. 'We do need to leave, but we also need a plausible story to stop the lawman coming after us. While you were checking I hadn't stolen off you, I was working on that story.'

'Then keep working on it because whether you've kept the lawman quiet or not, I'm taking my chances at Raw Creek.'

Tex stalked away. Jeff watched him leave then moved to follow him to the camp-fire, but he heard a noise to his side, perhaps a faint sliding of pebbles over pebbles. He stopped and looked to the shadows, seeing only the darkened outline of the scrub flickering in the light from the fire.

He stayed poised for a minute, breathing shallowly, then shrugged and moved off. He tried to dismiss the matter as being just a night animal, but when he reached the camp-fire he saw that three of the workers weren't there.

As he sat he didn't react other than to look at Tex, who was scowling, although he couldn't tell whether that was because he'd noticed that the men were missing or because of their argument. A few minutes later Abigail called out that dinner was ready and the missing men returned, each coming from a different direction.

None of them looked at him, but when the food had been dished out, he felt his neck burn. From the corner of his eye he looked to the side. One of the men, Dawson, was staring at him, but the moment he saw his interest he looked away and hunched over his meal.

Jeff started eating but not before he'd noticed that Tex was also watching Dawson.

CHAPTER 6

'We have to move on,' Jeff shouted to Cassidy, when he'd climbed up on to the wagon. 'It's sunup and I want to be in Raw Creek by sundown.'

Cassidy was the only person who was not yet ready to leave, but he continued to stand beside a blanket, the only remaining piece of property that hadn't been packed away.

'We can't leave,' he said. 'We're a man short: Dawson ain't around.'

Jeff gulped as the obvious thought hit him and to cover his concern he stood to check that everyone was in position.

Tex was up front with two men sitting beside him, shuffling on his seat and appearing enthusiastic to get moving. Todd was sitting on Jeff's wagon, the men on the last wagon were ready, and Abigail was on her buggy waiting to go. Aside from Samuel who was sitting on his horse staring into space, as he always did when there was work to be done, Cassidy was the only one dallying.

With the silence dragging on, Jeff reckoned he needed to say something.

'Who saw him last?' he asked.

Cassidy looked along the length of the convoy, but nobody replied for several seconds until Tex slowly stood.

'I took over his watch,' he said. 'He was fine then.'

'Hear anything untoward afterwards?'

'Nope, and neither did anybody else.' Tex looked around for confirmation and received a chorus of affirmative grunts.

Cassidy kicked at the ground with his hands on his hips, presumably hoping that Dawson would return and so save him from having to make a tough decision. After waiting for a minute, Jeff raised the reins.

'We can't wait for him,' he said. 'He's either left us or he's loitering somewhere. Either way, it's his problem. We're moving on.'

'Then you'll have to move on without me.' Cassidy kicked the blanket aside. 'Dawson's blanket is still curled up as if he left it in a hurry. I reckon something happened here last night.'

'Fine with me,' Tex shouted from the front and moved to head on out, but then was halted by Cassidy's strident demand.

'Nobody leaves. Look!' He pointed to a spot closer to the creek then hurried over to it and hunkered down.

With Cassidy not providing any further explanation, Jeff got down from the wagon. One by one everyone else joined him before sauntering over to find out what had interested the lawman while muttering to each other about the delay.

'This had better be important,' Jeff said when he joined Cassidy, 'because we sure as. . . .'

Jeff trailed off when he saw what had concerned Cassidy. A dark patch marred the sandy soil. It had dried so it was hard to tell what it was, but wetness had also been splattered on several stones and they hadn't dried letting him see that a considerable amount of blood had been shed here.

Worse, deep footprints were around the bloodstain and twin furrows headed to the creek.

It was impossible to prove what the furrows were but Jeff envisaged that someone had been hurt badly then dragged backwards to the water. He guessed the lawman had had the same thought, although he hoped that didn't include knowing who had done the dragging.

'I was right,' Cassidy said. 'Something bad happened here last night.'

'All the more reason to move on quickly,' Jeff said, standing rigidly to avoid looking at Tex.

'Agreed,' Cassidy said. He stood to scan the horizons. 'I expected trouble after Raw Creek, but it's not unexpected that it happened before.'

'We'll be more careful,' Jeff said. He turned to address the assembled group, who were all standing quietly and eyeing each other with concern now that the dangers they would face had become all too real. 'From now on nobody will be on their own and two men will be on guard at night.'

He received nods from everyone except Todd who was staring transfixed at the stain and Samuel who was idly looking elsewhere as if he hadn't even realized a man had died here.

'When you've moved out,' Cassidy said, 'I'll scout downriver and see if I can find his body. I'll catch up with you later.'

With that comment he headed to his horse. Everybody was slow to disband with most muttering with concern about what had happened.

Jeff wasn't surprised that Tex remained. He waited until everyone was out of earshot.

'Is he dead?' he whispered, having decided that an admonishment would be ignored.

'Knife went clean through him,' Tex said, smirking. 'If that didn't do it, then drowning sure did.'

Jeff nodded. 'You sure he was the only one taking too much of an interest in the first wagon?'

'They'd all better hope he was the only one.' Tex turned to head to his wagon. 'Because I'll kill every one of them if I have to.'

'Raw Creek,' Patrick shouted out, 'one mile after the rise.'

Cassidy looked ahead searching for his first sight of the town. He had never been to Raw Creek before but he had heard it was a rough town in keeping with its location on the edge of the inhospitable Barren Plains.

Earlier he'd found Dawson's body five miles downriver from their camp. He'd been stabbed. It was an uncomfortable thought that he'd been killed a dozen yards away from his sleeping companions and while somebody had been on watch.

If the killer had been a lone scavenger, he'd have expected him to scavenge, but nothing was missing. If Blake had been responsible, he'd have expected him to then attack them all. So Cassidy surmised that either Blake was trying to unnerve them by picking them off one by one, or the killer was someone from the convoy.

The latter reason was an unlikely explanation as the journey had been a quiet one. The potential danger they would face had concentrated everyone's minds and kept at bay the usual bickering and fights. Even so, Patrick had hired a rough collection of men and it was possible that someone had risked killing even when a lawman was with them.

Despite brooding on the issue he was no nearer to deciding what he thought had happened when he crested the rise and caught his first sight of Raw Creek.

That sight drove away all thoughts of Dawson's death.

Tendrils of smoke were spiralling up from the dozen or so buildings that comprised the town. That wasn't unusual even in the warmth of the late afternoon, but every house had smoke rising from it and even from a mile away, Cassidy saw that the buildings themselves were blackened and derelict.

He doubled-back to the convoy and with a raised hand ordered everyone to halt. Then he rode along to Patrick.

'We'll check out the town first,' he said.

Patrick stood to look ahead, peering with his eyes narrowed at the town, then nodded. He commandeered Samuel's horse after treating him to a barked demand to dismount and together they rode towards town. Long before they reached the buildings Cassidy saw that he had been right.

The town had been razed to the ground.

'Blake Kelly,' Patrick murmured.

'Could be, and recently with the look of it. Be careful. He could still be here.'

'Makes you wonder why he killed only Dawson if he had the firepower to wipe out a whole town.'

Cassidy shrugged, keeping his thoughts to himself on the possibility of that death being the responsibility of someone within their group and instead concentrated on looking out for trouble.

They reached the edge of town without seeing any sign of life. Here the stench of burning was cloying and eye-watering. Whoever had caused this devastation had been thorough, having torched every building.

Strangely they had yet to see a body and so Cassidy wondered if he'd jumped to the wrong conclusion. This could have been an accident. He was turning to Patrick to offer this thought when a gunshot rang out.

Cassidy couldn't tell where the shot had come from, or where it had been aimed, but he didn't take any chances. He leapt down off his horse. Patrick followed him and together they scurried into hiding behind the remnants of the nearest building.

They hunkered down behind a wall that had been shortened to about four feet high, the wood being charred so deeply that Cassidy reckoned a mere touch would knock it over.

'This is poor cover,' Patrick said, matching his thoughts. 'A well-aimed bullet could go straight through this and hit us.'

'Then we have to make sure nobody gets a chance to fire one.' Cassidy raised himself to look over the top of the wall, seeing nothing move aside from the smoke spreading down the road.

Patrick raised himself then pointed. 'Stay here. I'll take the other side of the road and get a different angle.'

Cassidy slapped his back then counted down on his fingers. The moment Patrick took his cue to head out into the road running doubled over, he fired over the top of the wall at a dangling strip of wood swaying precariously in the breeze on a building twenty yards away. His first shot cannoned off the wood and the second sent it to the ground, where it disintegrated in a puff of ash.

He was looking for another safe target when Patrick rolled into hiding. He matched Cassidy's stance by peering over the top of the short wall. Then they waited. Long moments passed where Cassidy could hear only the wind whipping around the buildings and the occasional pop of wood that was still burning.

When he judged that whoever was out there wouldn't take the initiative, he hollered out.

'You out there,' he called, 'hold your fire.'

By way of an answer a gunshot blasted. Cassidy ducked, as did Patrick. They stayed down, but when a second and a third crack of gunfire tore out, Cassidy looked at Patrick, who shrugged.

'Either he's got a mighty bad aim,' Patrick called, 'or those shots weren't meant for us.'

'Or,' Cassidy said, standing, 'they were to get our attention.'

He stood and paced out into the road. Another gunshot sounded and this time Cassidy saw a puff of smoke ripple up from within the wrecked remnants of the last building on the road.

He pointed and in response Patrick stood then joined him in walking towards it. Cassidy didn't try to walk quietly and his hunch turned out to be right when someone spoke up from within the building.

'I've got one bullet left,' a voice screeched. 'Tell me you've come to help or I'll use it.'

'We are here to help,' Cassidy said. 'I'm Sheriff Cassidy Yates.'

Then he stepped up to the building to peer over the heap of burnt wood and saw that the survivor's comment hadn't been a threat.

If he had one bullet left, he was saving it for himself.

CHAPTER 7

Wilbur Frost was the only one survivor of the Raw Creek massacre, but Jeff reckoned that was only a temporary state of affairs.

Wilbur was so badly burnt even the hard-nosed workers balked at approaching him and rather than help, they were more eager to join Cassidy in the potentially dangerous task of scouting around.

So Abigail sat with him and did what she could. Jeff stayed with her and helped by passing her ripped-up cloth to use as bandages and ferrying water from the wagons.

As she worked, Abigail encouraged Wilbur to talk to take his mind off the pain. On first seeing him Jeff had thought he'd been trapped in a burning building, but the truth was more horrific.

The previous night, while the townsfolk slept, the Dark Riders had come and before anyone had been able to mount a defence, they had seized control of the town. The few who had fought back had been shot and once the raiders had taken whatever valuables they could find, the townsfolk had been herded back into the buildings. Then the doors and windows had been nailed up, the buildings torched, and they'd been left to die in their fiery prisons.

Wilbur was the only lucky one, although Jeff doubted that was the right way to look at it.

With his tale complete, Abigail subtly steered him round to discussing her own problem.

'Has anyone new passed through town recently?' she asked.

'Just the Dark Riders,' Wilbur said.

'Heard of anyone else? Such as a man and a woman, Jane and Ethan Norton. They were planning to prospect for silver in the Barren Plains.'

'Plenty of people make that trip. Some even come back.'

'I know but—'

'Enough, Abigail,' Jeff said using a gentle tone. 'When Wilbur's comfortable and he can think straight you can question him some more about what happened to Jane.'

Abigail pouted, looking as if she'd argue but then provided a reluctant nod.

'Try to rest, Wilbur,' she said, patting his arm on one of the few non-reddened spots, 'and call for me if there's anything I can do.'

He gulped and offered a tentative smile through his cracked and blistered lips.

'Is there anything you can do?'

Abigail's wince clearly showed she couldn't find an answer.

'Just rest,' she urged, then stood. With none of the others having returned yet she paced away from the ruined house to stand in the road.

Jeff joined her and after they'd stood for a while, he noted that this was the first time they'd been alone together, but with the difficult task of helping Wilbur over for now, standing quietly made him just as uneasy. They looked away from each other while he searched for something to say, but nothing would come, so he moved to check out the wagons.

Then he noticed that Tex had stayed behind. He was leaning against the lead wagon, unsubtly standing in the same position where Cassidy had seen him acting suspiciously yesterday.

Jeff was minded to tell him to move to avoid the risk of exposing them, but then he noticed that Abigail's shoulders were shaking and he heard the sobs she was trying to suppress.

'Don't cry,' he said joining her. 'Other survivors could be hiding out there and they might have seen your sister.'

'I know,' she said, then fought to stop herself crying by throwing back her head and looking skywards. 'But even if they have, her dream of coming here to start a new life could have ended with her being killed horribly.'

She sobbed again then wrapped her arms around her chest and stamped a foot as she fought to control her sadness and irritation.

'You have no reason to suppose Blake Kelly has found your sister.' He smiled and she looked at him, pleading with her eyes for him to offer more comfort, but he couldn't think of a reason why he might be right and so with a shrug he ended his support lamely. 'She could still be safe.'

'Maybe she could, but with those Dark Riders out there, she won't be safe for long, even if she's survived in the Barren Plains. And that's provided those prospectors were who they said they were and they didn't kill her outside Carmon.'

'That's a mighty lot of surmising. You start thinking like that and you won't ever find her.'

She fought back her snuffles for long enough to smile.

'I'll try, but it's been months since I last saw her and I can't help but get upset about it.' She looked towards the distant spire of rock that marked Bleak Point, visible as a faint outline on the horizon, and when she spoke again she sounded calmer. 'You know the region we're heading into. Do you think she could still be alive?'

Jeff thought about the map in his pocket, which represented the sum total of his knowledge of the Barren Plains. He was minded to lie, but he figured she deserved better than that.

'It's an inhospitable place and that works two ways. It's hard for decent people to survive, but it ain't much easier on the men who prey on those decent people.'

Jeff reckoned he'd stated only common sense and hadn't raised her hopes with any untruths. But he was pleased when his comment made her wipe her eyes with a quick swipe that said she was determined not to weep again. Then they settled down outside the house in which Wilbur was resting.

An hour later everyone had returned. Cassidy had left with the two youngest members so he could keep watch on them. Todd looked suitably sobered and even Samuel had an expression that was so grim Jeff didn't need to hear what they'd found.

The others had the same news to relay. Wilbur was the only survivor. The rest had either been locked in the buildings then burned to death, or had fled for their lives then been gunned down.

If any had escaped, they hadn't returned.

Cassidy listened to the tales, then provided the only good news he could find in this sorry sequence of events.

'At least Blake Kelly appears to have gone,' he said with a cheerful tone that Jeff presumed was false as he tried to get everyone feeling positive and to stop dwelling on their predicament. He pointed at the building where Wilbur was lying. 'And how is our newest convoy member?'

'Doing as well as possible,' Abigail said. 'But he's burnt real bad. I don't think he's fit enough to be left alone here, or for that matter to join the convoy.'

Cassidy frowned, acknowledging the unspoken problem this gave them.

'Did he see the previous convoy pass through?'

Abigail shrugged and Jeff was pleased that Cassidy was looking at her so that he didn't see him wince. He hadn't asked about the convoy and Patrick Carey would have done that.

'He's in a poor way,' Jeff said, covering himself. 'Questioning him wasn't easy.'

Cassidy nodded then headed over to the building to sit with Wilbur. He ducked down, but within moments he stood and returned shaking his head.

Everyone stayed quiet and bowed their heads. After a respectful silence, Cassidy issued commands that gave everybody a specific task, ensuring that nobody had enough free time to get worried.

Abigail supervised the youngest members in foraging for unburnt wood to use on the journey ahead. One man manoeuvred the wagons into the centre of town while a detail left to dig graves.

As even Tex had volunteered for this task Jeff joined him, planning to discuss how they'd get away from the lawman now that they couldn't claim they'd learnt something here. But Cassidy beckoned for him to stay.

'We have to decide where we'll go now,' he said. 'With the Dark Riders out there, I don't want to risk Abigail's life, or Todd's, Samuel's and everyone else's for that matter.'

Jeff reckoned Cassidy was sounding him out on the idea he'd suggested last night, but to avoid appearing too eager he swung round to watch the grave-digging detail while rubbing his chin.

'You may have no choice but to risk everyone's lives,' he said. 'If Blake killed Dawson, even going back the way we came will be dangerous.'

'That's a fair point. So are you saying we should carry on?'

'Some of us should. I reckon our best option is the one I suggested last night. We split up. Mike and I will get Abigail, Todd and Samuel to safety at Carmon. The rest knew the dangers when I hired them and they can carry on to Bleak Point with you. If they complain, I'll double their wages.'

Cassidy firmed his jaw while he considered.

'With fewer men I'll have to stay with the convoy and wait for Blake to come looking for me.' Cassidy waited until Jeff nodded before continuing 'So I need more firepower. Mike must stay.'

To avoid Cassidy seeing his concern, Jeff looked away to pick out Tex, who was digging. He was minded to agree and let Tex sort out his own problems, but it'd probably be a violent way, and even if he just slunk away in the night it would raise questions he was trying to avoid.

'He could, but a man, a woman and two lads could attract Blake.' He rocked his head from side to side as if were considering. 'Perhaps we should let Mike decide what he wants to do.'

'I can't,' Cassidy said, his sterner tone alerting Jeff to the problem ahead. 'I need him. If I can't take him with me, I can't let you go back.'

Jeff winced. He couldn't think of a valid excuse for Tex staying with him when Cassidy was heading in the most dangerous direction, so he provided the answer he reckoned Patrick Carey would have given.

'And if I don't go back, you can't go on. So I guess we stay here.'

'I guess we do,' Cassidy said.

*

Jeff had slept for only a few fitful hours when Cassidy woke him.

Cassidy had ensured they followed the instructions he had given that morning by keeping two people on watch at all times. Abigail had demanded to be included and she was sharing Jeff's watch. She went over to the first building on the opposite end of town and paced back and forth.

Jeff stretched then began his watch by sitting on the wall of what, from the half-burnt sign he saw lying on the ground, had once been a stable. The wagons were stretched out down the road and snores were arising from the most solid of the ruins where everyone had settled down for the night.

Sunup was several hours away and a chill wind was rustling the sparse scrub. With the fire being just a dull glow outside the sleeping area, the main light came from the rising crescent moon, which bathed the undulating scrub in a harsh light that did nothing to cheer Jeff.

With there being only one more watch after his, he figured he wouldn't be sleeping again as he'd yet to come up with an idea to break the impasse.

When they'd retired Cassidy had still been reluctant to risk Abigail's life by moving on into the Barren Plains, but neither would he accept Jeff's solution. They hadn't brought anyone into their deliberations and as they'd arrived late in the day nobody had questioned their reasoning for staying, but come tomorrow that would change.

That thought reminded Jeff of Tex's ultimatum. Tex had taken the first duty and if he still had the same plans, he would have expected him to take advantage of his time alone, but when he'd been woken up, Tex was still with them. Despite that he headed to the lead wagon and on the opposite side to Abigail he examined the supplies.

The ropes appeared slacker than they had been before so he lifted one to peer at the cargo. With an outstretched hand he pushed the crate that was lying on their haul. He couldn't move it aside to reach the sack beneath, but although he was unsure in the poor light, the sack appeared flatter than the last time he'd seen it back at the depot.

He leaned further in, trying to reach the sack, then raised himself aiming to slip on to the back of the wagon.

A hand slapped down on his back.

'What you doing?' Tex grunted in his ear.

Jeff flinched then took deep breaths to quieten his heart before he rocked down on to his heels and turned to face him.

'You know what I was doing,' he said then smiled as he remembered what Tex had said yesterday. 'I'm checking you haven't been sneaking into the sacks and helping yourself to my share.'

'I haven't. I'd have split the haul fairly and left earlier, but Cassidy was on duty after me and I didn't want to risk sneaking away while he was snooping around. But I can leave when you're keeping lookout.'

'What excuse can I give?'

'Don't care.'

Jeff sneered. 'Then I'll tell everyone you're a yellow-belly and you ran to save your hide.'

Tex's eyes narrowed and he leaned forward as if he was preparing to confront him, but then he gave a dismissive wave.

'Tell them what you want. As long as I don't have to suffer your whining, I'll be happy.'

Jeff considered. If Tex left, it would solve one problem, but he was unsure if it would improve the chances of Cassidy letting him leave with Abigail while he carried on into the Barren Plains. But whichever option Cassidy chose, he figured he'd settle for not having to see his murderous partner again.

'Can't say I'm sad we're parting company either. I hope they find you and stretch your neck.'

Tex snorted a laugh. 'Same for you.'

Tex slapped a hand on the wagon, aiming to climb on to it and split their haul, but, as he raised himself, Jeff heard a footfall and from the corner of his eye he saw movement. He turned towards that movement but saw only the scrub. Still, he felt sure he'd seen and heard someone move.

'Wait!' he said, raising his voice more than he'd wanted to.

'Be quiet,' Tex muttered swinging round to face him. 'Wake the others and you'll be the first to die.'

'Quit the threats. Somebody's out there.'

'Abigail?'

'No. She's behind us.'

Tex opened his mouth to continue arguing, but another footfall sounded and this time it was loud enough for Tex to hear. He stood beside Jeff, looking away from town.

'Somebody is out there, snooping around. I knew someone else had heard us talking.' Tex snorted. 'I'll make him regret that.'

Tex's hand jerked towards his belt, but Jeff heard another footfall, this time coming from twenty yards to the side of the previous ones. He slapped a hand on his arm, halting his movement.

'You won't. Two men are out there, maybe more.'

Tex flinched, the thought that had dawned on Jeff hitting him.

'Blake Kelly?' he murmured.

Jeff nodded and so they backed away a pace to stand against the wagon. Both men faced the scrub looking for the first sign of movement that would herald an attack. For long moments all was quiet.

Then the Dark Riders came.

First one man, then a second and a third rose from the scrub, around ten yards away. Each man was clad in black. They stood as silent sentinels, watching them, their features shrouded in the gloom. Then a fourth man stood and delivered an overarm gesture.

In response the three other men hunched over but Jeff and Tex didn't wait to see what the gesture had meant. They dropped to their knees, the movement saving them from the simultaneous gunshots that tore into the wagon's sideboards. They rolled beneath the wagon and on hands and feet scrambled underneath it to reach the other side.

Jeff emerged to see Abigail vault into the end building then peer out while from the building where the rest were sleeping, first Cassidy then the other men emerged. They were all armed, proving they'd slept with one hand on a gun.

'It's Blake,' Jeff reported. 'The Dark Riders are attacking.'

Cassidy nodded then gestured to the men to take up positions at each end of the convoy and between the wagons. Jeff was closest to the gap between the first and second wagon so he slipped between them and hurried to the other side.

When he emerged he picked out the men in the scrub as they moved to new positions. A shot blasted out from one of the defenders and taking that as his cue, Jeff joined him in firing at the moving targets.

In the same silent way that they'd arrived, as one the men ducked into the scrub, taking them from view in an instant. Several men still tore out wild shots into the undergrowth until Cassidy urged them to save their bullets.

Then they waited, staring into the night and waiting for the first person to show himself. Time passed slowly, but none of the Dark Riders reappeared.

Jeff wondered if the first attack had been a ruse to draw them to this side of town and so he turned and set off, aiming to investigate on the other side of the wagons. He'd walked for a single pace when he barged into the person creeping up on him from behind. A cry tore from his lips as he and the other person went down entangled.

Jeff's gun got caught up beneath him and he was struggling to free it when he heard a squeak, a sound that was more feminine than he'd have expected one of the Dark Riders to make. Then he felt the soft body beneath him and realized his apparent assailant was Abigail.

With an embarrassed cough, he got to his feet and dragged her up with him, then offered her a smile that she couldn't see in the dark.

'Everything fine out your way?' he asked, his voice gruff as he struggled to find something to say.

'I haven't seen anybody yet,' she said, her tone flustered. 'I thought I'd be safer with you.'

'Until I knocked you down.'

'Even then,' she said.

Jeff narrowed his eyes, wishing now that it wasn't dark so he could see her expression and perhaps work out why she had said something so intriguing. But he figured if it did mean what he hoped it meant she might not have said it in the dark.

Then he shook himself, deciding he'd been mistaken. They'd hardly spoken until today and she'd spent most of her time with Cassidy.

'Stay here and look that way,' he said, pointing. 'I'll look the other way.'

He patted her shoulder then turned to look at the scrub. While he'd been distracted the rising moon had increased the light level, but he could still see only the top of the scrub. So he settled down to wait.

Slowly the sky below the moon gathered its own crescent of light and with each increase in the light level he became more confident that the Dark Riders wouldn't come back tonight.

Presently Cassidy joined him, walking in full view along the side of the wagons.

'So they've decided not to attack,' he said.

'We were more prepared than the townsfolk,' Jeff said. 'Perhaps Blake likes only easy targets.'

'Then we'll make sure he never gets one.'

Cassidy gave Abigail an encouraging smile then picked out two men to join him in scouting around. One of those men was Tex and, as he left, he cast dark glances at Jeff that appeared to say he blamed him for the fact he wouldn't be able to sneak away unseen now.

While the men were away Jeff expected that only Tex would return and that he'd explain the demise of the others as being Blake's doing before he embarked on a mission to kill them all. But all three men returned and their reports confirmed the situation. Numerous footprints were dotted around showing they'd been watched for some time, but the Dark Riders had gone.

Cassidy listened to their reports. Then, with his shoulders hunched and with the air of a man with a lot on his mind, he withdrew to stand beside the fire. He rested a raised foot on a short wall and put his weight on his knee then looked over his shoulder at Jeff.

'He wants a word,' Abigail said, leaning towards

him. 'Make sure it's the right one.'

Jeff didn't ask what she meant although he reckoned she was saying that despite this attack she wanted to head on into the Barren Plains. He nodded then headed over to join Cassidy.

'Blake and his Dark Riders are out there,' Cassidy said, looking beyond the fire. 'They could be anywhere. Going back could be as dangerous as going on.'

'It could,' Jeff said cautiously. 'Except Blake has taken refuge in the Barren Plains and only ventures out for these raids. Going on is the more dangerous option.'

'That's right.' Cassidy cleared his throat. 'And for that reason I'm agreeing with your plan. You and Mike will get Abigail and the two lads to safety. I'll press on to Bleak Point with the rest.'

'I won't let you down,' Jeff said, fighting to keep his voice level and not betray his relief.

'But I'll only task you with that duty if you answer one question.' Cassidy turned to look at him for the first time. 'What are you and Mike up to?'

Jeff gulped, forcing his expression to remain fixed.

'What do you mean?'

Cassidy narrowed his eyes while he searched Jeff's eyes.

'I don't know, but you do. Something's amiss and I can't figure out what it is, but faced with the enormity of what happened here and the dangers ahead, I don't know if it's important. So tell me what you're doing and it'll go no further.' Cassidy waited, but Jeff's mind was whirling too much for him to answer. 'Are you overcharging the miners? Is there something in those supplies you don't want me to see? Was the previous convoy ferrying something you don't want me to know about?'

Jeff breathed a sigh of relief. Cassidy only thought he was up to no good in the normal way a man like Patrick Carey might behave.

'There are some things it's better for a lawman not to know,' he said with a joking tone. 'It might get him worried, if you know what I mean, but will you accept my word that it's nothing serious?'

Jeff smiled, hoping Cassidy wouldn't want more information as he didn't think he could create a convincing lie. Cassidy looked away to consider Samuel and Todd then Abigail. He provided a reluctant nod.

'Perhaps there's too much going on to worry about that sort of thing. I'll trust you.' Cassidy placed his raised foot on the ground and sighed. 'But I reckon Abigail will be more concerned about this plan than I am.'

Cassidy wasn't wrong.

When they headed back to the wagons to give everyone their decision, Abigail's reaction was worse than Jeff had feared. She opened her mouth wide in incredulity, tears brimmed, and worst of all she shot him a wounded look.

Feeling guilty because he'd only suggested his plan so that he could escape with the stolen haul while avoiding Blake, he couldn't meet her eye. Instead, he let Cassidy deal with her anger while he joined Tex.

'What's she crying about?' Tex asked.

'I was saving her life and yours,' Jeff said. 'We're leaving the convoy with no questions asked and no problems left behind.'

'Don't matter to me. I was leaving anyhow.' Tex headed off to stand beside the lead wagon where as usual he eyed everyone with suspicion.

The next hour was tense as everyone prepared to depart. By sunup they were ready. Jeff tethered Abigail's spare horse to the back of her buggy while she got on the seat. Todd, Samuel and Tex mounted up alongside them.

On the back of the buggy was Abigail's belongings and supplies for the journey. Underneath them was the stolen haul that Tex had transferred from the wagon when Cassidy had been explaining the situation to Abigail.

She hadn't brought much more than a change of clothing and the supplies filled only a single sack, but the haul ensured they created a suspiciously large mound. So when Jeff joined her on the buggy he was eager to get out of the lawman's sight quickly.

'Cassidy,' he called out, 'turning our backs on the Barren Plains is rough on Abigail. I don't want to make this any harder for her. Good luck.'

He raised the reins and hurried the buggy off through the rows of derelict buildings. His neck burned in expectation of Cassidy calling them back and then discovering their secret, but he moved away from town without hearing anything.

When he reached the rise where he'd first seen that the town had been burnt to the ground he stopped and looked back.

Cassidy was leading the convoy into the Barren Plains at a steady pace. Jeff allowed himself a sigh of relief then gave Abigail a smile that she didn't return.

'I thought you understood that I had to find Jane,' she said, glaring at him. 'I thought you cared about me. I thought you were different. But you let me down.'

'And not just you,' Jeff said, urging the horses to move on.

CHAPTER 8

Sundown was an hour away when Jeff's group reached the spot beside the creek where they'd camped the previous night. They'd seen no sign of Blake Kelly and the Dark Riders.

As he couldn't remember passing any other suitable locations nearby he suggested they stopped here. Everyone was tired after last night's mainly sleepless sojourn, so in the lee of a tangle of boulders they halted.

Abigail was still in a sullen mood and the rest of Jeff's companions were just as grumpy.

Samuel was always unhappy, and he could understand Todd's attitude. He had acquitted himself well during the journey to Raw Creek and was clearly looking forward to proving himself amongst the men, but being judged to be someone who needed protecting had knocked him back.

Tex's demeanour was a mystery to him, but while Abigail and Todd prepared a fire and Samuel mooched around, for the first time since leaving Raw

Creek he found himself alone with him. Tex didn't waste a moment in explaining himself.

'This sure is a damn fool plan,' he barked.

'It ain't,' Jeff said. He drew Tex behind a boulder so the others wouldn't overhear what, from the anger in Tex's eyes, he was sure would be a tense argument. 'But why should it worry you? You wanted to leave the convoy before morning. You did. Now you can slip away when you want to while I take them back to Carmon. Then I can disappear too and everyone will think we both came to a bad end in the Barren Plains.'

'You'll never reach Carmon. Somebody will have missed Patrick Carey by now and Marshal McCoy must know we're not near Monotony. He's sure to follow up Cassidy's theory that Blake is out here.'

'Then I'll take a different route and avoid him,' Jeff snapped. In truth, he hadn't considered that Marshal McCoy could be heading towards them and his tone must have betrayed that uncertainty because Tex snorted then glanced at the knife while grinning with malevolence.

'No more excuses, Jeff. You've given me no choice but to kill them all before one of them sees what's in the buggy.'

'You don't have to kill again,' Jeff murmured, aghast. 'Leave now. I'll make sure nobody sees my share and no matter what happens, I won't help McCoy find you.'

Tex's stern expression said he wouldn't risk himself when he could easily kill their charges. Jeff opened his mouth to continue trying to persuade him to be reasonable, but then said nothing when Todd came running around the side of the boulder.

'You have to come,' Todd demanded. 'Abigail's gone.'

'Where? When?' Jeff asked.

Todd didn't get the chance to answer when, with an angry oath, Tex barged him to the ground and ran off around the boulder. Jeff got to his feet and followed. She'd left on her spare horse so the thought that had concerned Tex probably hadn't occurred. Tex still hurried to the buggy and looked over the backboard.

Jeff turned towards the setting sun, unconcerned about the possibility of her having stolen their haul. With a hand to his brow he saw a dispersing dust cloud back along the route they'd taken from Raw Creek.

'She just saved her life,' Tex said, then edged his hand to the hilt of his knife while looking at Todd and Samuel, a motion that said even if she had, he couldn't make the same claim for the others.

'Todd,' Jeff said before Tex could act, 'Samuel, get her back.'

Todd nodded and moved to his horse, but acting in a typical fashion Samuel stood slouched while staring vacantly in the direction she'd gone. With him not moving, it was left for Todd to double-back then grab his arm and direct him to his horse.

'Do I have to go?' Samuel muttered, digging in his heels and extricating his arm from Todd's grip. He gave Jeff an aggrieved look that asked for clemency. 'It'll get dark soon and I'm tired.'

'Go!' Jeff snapped.

'Yeah,' Tex said, 'chase after her as if your life depended on it.'

Jeff didn't add that leaving now really would save his life, but the stern nature of their demands had the desired effect and he sloped off after Todd. Jeff waited until both lads were riding away before he turned to Tex.

'Take your half and go,' he said. 'I'll excuse you and take them back to Carmon. You can take your own chances.'

'I will,' Tex said, smirking, 'but you know that's not the way this was ever going to end, don't you? Only one of us would leave and that man would take all the money. Now we decide who that man is.'

Tex moved his jacket aside to free both his gun and knife.

'Twenty dollars was enough for me,' Jeff said, raising his hands and taking a slow pace backwards, 'so I was content with a twelfth and then a half. We don't have to fight for it all.'

Tex shrugged. 'Maybe we don't. Maybe I should wait for Todd and Samuel to bring Abigail back and then before I go I can enjoy myself with—'

'Enough!' Jeff demanded. 'You ain't hurting them and if the only way I can stop you is to kill you, so be it.'

Tex snorted a harsh laugh. 'Now you're talking sense.'

While keeping his gaze set on Jeff, Tex removed a knife from his boot and threw it to the ground at Jeff's feet. Then he placed his other hand in position to unhook his gunbelt.

Getting his meaning that they should decide their argument without guns, Jeff matched Tex's movement. He unhooked his belt then joined Tex in holding it at arm's length then throwing it to the side and away from the buggy. Then he knelt to pick up the knife. As he'd expected it had a shorter blade than the long cruel knife Tex was brandishing and with Tex's proven cutting skills he had the advantage.

Despite his slim chances, Jeff accepted Tex was right. He had probably always known that he would ultimately face this battle.

He hefted the knife on his palm, getting used to its weight and feel. He'd never had to defend himself like this before and his greenness must have been obvious because with a confident swagger Tex moved towards him.

To give himself time to think through his tactics Jeff crouched forward with the knife thrust out pointing at Tex then backed away towards the buggy. Tex kept his knife held upwards beside his cheek ensuring that when Jeff looked at the blade he also saw him grinning with confidence.

'Come on,' Jeff said, beckoning Tex on in a suitably arrogant manner.

'You're the one backing away,' Tex said, smirking. 'But there's nowhere to run.'

Jeff slipped around the front of the buggy and his

new position let him confirm that Tex was right. There was nothing nearby other than the creek and the few large boulders, which were all too smooth to climb easily.

He doubted he could reach the horse. He had to find an advantage and so when he reached the other side of the buggy he ran on for two paces then used his momentum to vault up onto the buggy. He went to his knees beside the sacks then raised himself and planted a foot on the top of the pile.

'You want the money,' he shouted down at Tex, thrusting his chin high with bravado while pointing down at the haul, 'you come up here and get it.'

Tex stopped at the corner of the buggy then looked for the best place to climb up, but the buggy was so small Jeff could probably reach him with the blade no matter which side he tried.

'I'm in no hurry,' Tex said. He backed away for a pace and adopted a casual stance. 'I can wait until the others return and then deal with you all together.'

Jeff winced, accepting that Tex could wait him out. So he shrugged to appear defeated. Then one-handed he grabbed the topmost sack containing half their stolen bills and threw it at Tex.

Tex batted the sack aside, but Jeff followed through with the second sack. This one missed Tex by several feet. Laughing mockingly, Tex moved in a pace, but for the last sack, the one containing the heavier valuables, Jeff dropped the knife then hefted the weighty sack above his head.

Tex stopped in his tracks and raised an arm in a warding-off gesture but he was too late. Jeff launched the sack at Tex with all his strength. It hit him in the upper chest and wrapped itself around his body and head then knocked him backwards for a pace before he fell.

Jeff gave him no time to recover. He scooped up the knife then leapt down. As Tex floundered, he landed on the ground beside him. Before Tex could extricate himself from the sack, Jeff leapt on him then bore down with his chest, trapping Tex beneath the sack and pinning him to the ground.

Tex struggled, kicking out, but he couldn't reach Jeff's legs and move him.

'Relent,' Jeff shouted. He placed his hands on the sack at the place where he judged Tex's head was and pressed down. 'I don't want to kill you. You can still leave with half of all this.'

Tex's muffled oaths and grunts left Jeff in no doubt that he wasn't interested in the offer. Then Tex managed to slip his left hand out from under the sack and grab the wrist of Jeff's knife hand. Fingers dug into the muscle, forcing Jeff to release his pressure on the sack.

Tex took advantage of his weakness and pushed upwards, throwing Jeff off him. Jeff landed on his side with the entangled sack ensuring Tex rolled towards him.

To stop Tex turning the tables and pinning him down, Jeff kicked and scrambled and fought his way out from the sack then tried to pull himself away from Tex's grip. But he failed and so Jeff's pulling only succeeded in making the two men roll over and over each other.

Tex still held Jeff's knife hand but Tex's knife was caught in the sack. That situation couldn't continue for long and sure enough when Jeff next found himself on his back with Tex looming over him Tex steadied himself then with a roar of triumph tore the knife from the burlap.

The shredded sack fell away leaving the knife held above him, glinting red with promised malice in the low sunlight. Then it came slicing down. Jeff jerked his head to the side and the knife parted hair before it stuck into the soft earth.

Tex snorted with irritation then tore the knife from the dirt, but by the time he'd raised it again Jeff had squirmed away from Tex's grip. On his knees Jeff swung round to face him.

They got to their feet, all the time watching the other. With their arms thrust out before them they closed on each other, as Tex had originally intended.

Knives jerked forward, thrust, sliced, but each lunge missed its intended target by several feet as each man sought an opening without risking himself.

Jeff's initial success had taken some of the arrogance from Tex's eyes, but Jeff judged that as soon as he regained his confidence, he would attempt a murderous assault that with his greater strength and skill was sure to succeed.

So while he still had a chance Jeff advanced on Tex. This made him back away using one steady pace at a time. Jeff speeded his approach and Tex matched his pace, but that proved to have been a ploy when Tex dug in a heel then jerked forward and slashed around with a long swipe of the blade.

Sharp pain tore through Jeff's left forearm as the knife found flesh. Drops of dark blood dripped to the dirt.

'First blood,' Tex said, smirking. 'I'll get the last too.'

Tex lunged and this time Jeff was quick enough to dance backwards and the knife whistled through air. But he came at him again, and then again and again, his attacks relentless. One blow sliced through a sleeve, but missed skin; another came low and nicked his leg.

Jeff continued to back away, no longer aware of where he was as his world contracted to Tex's flashing knife and his attempts to avoid it. He gave no thought to trying to blood Tex.

Another thrust came and in a desperate move Jeff darted his hand in to meet the knife. The two knives clinked together and caught at the hilt.

Each man strained to push the other away. Jeff rocked backwards as Tex bore down on him, his trailing foot slipping backwards. Then he found solid footing and slowly reversed the movement, raising himself to his full height then pushing down and making Tex double over backwards. Their eyes met and in Tex's wide-eyed gaze Jeff thought he saw a hint of fear.

Heartened, Jeff redoubled his efforts, but in

response Tex strained harder. For a moment neither man was able to move, all their concentration being on the knives, but then with a painful jerk, Jeff's wrist gave way.

He staggered sideways. The knives scythed away from each other, the pressure each man had put on the blades making them impossible to control and in a spot of luck Jeff's knife bit into Tex's knuckle.

Blood sprayed. A cry of pain rent the air.

Taking advantage Jeff lunged aiming to stick Tex with a lethal blow to his chest. But as he stepped forward he saw for the first time the sack on the ground, their pacing having moved them in a circle. He was too late to avoid it. His foot became caught in the burlap and turned his lunge into a forward roll.

He lay sprawled at Tex's feet, his own knife tumbling from his weakened hand, his body exposed for a killing blow. He looked up to see Tex passing the knife over to his uninjured hand.

With only a moment to react before Tex slammed the knife down into his chest, Jeff lunged for Tex's dangling and wounded hand. He gripped it, grinding the knuckles.

Tex screeched as wetness oozed through Jeff's fingers then tore himself away. Blood flew from his hand, the pain making him release the knife. It dropped and slapped against Jeff's chest, luckily hilt first.

Tex staggered away wringing his hand, but he didn't get far when Jeff looped a raised leg around his knee and brought him down. Then he rolled to his feet, scooping up Tex's knife, and loomed over the sprawling man.

Tex was still in too much pain to pay attention to him. So Jeff kicked him on to his back then dropped to his knees and thrust the knife up under his chin. When he'd started the motion he had intended to slice him a new smile in the way Tex would have cut him, but at the last moment he stayed his hand and stopped with the knife pressed against flesh.

'Relent,' he said. For emphasis he pushed the knife. The point pricked skin. Blood flowed over cold metal. 'Second and last chance.'

'Never,' Tex muttered through clenched teeth. Then he tensed, stealing himself for the killing thrust.

Jeff flexed his arm as he prepared to kill Tex in cold blood, something his unwelcome partner would never have balked at doing.

That thought decided it for Jeff.

He relaxed, slipped the knife away from Tex's neck, then rolled back on to his haunches.

'I ain't killing you,' he said.

Tex sneered. 'I knew you didn't have the guts.'

'I've got the guts to kill a man who might kill me, but not to stick a man I've beaten, even when he's a murderous varmint like you are.'

Tex waited for the treachery he clearly expected, but when Jeff didn't move he got to his knees then adopted Jeff's posture.

'And you expect me to thank you?'

'I know exactly how you'll repay me. You'll scurry

into hiding like the snake you are, but then you'll find me and hound me until you get everything. And you won't show me the mercy I showed you.' Jeff stood. 'So I won't give you a reason to come after me.'

Tex stood. He glanced at the knife in Jeff's hand then darted his gaze around until he saw the other knife.

'You're going to kill me, after all,' he said, shuffling a half-pace towards the knife, 'and take all the money, aren't you?'

'No.' Jeff waited until Tex moved towards the knife again before he made his offer. 'You can have it all.'

Tex stopped and narrowed his eyes, clearly not having expected this offer. He glanced at the nearest sack then shook his head.

'What kind of twisted trick are you playing?'

'None. Take every last cent then run. And keep on running until the law finds you and strings you up or you choke on all those bills. I don't want any of it.'

'I don't believe you,' Tex said, although he moved away from the knife and shuffled towards the sacks. He placed his uninjured hand on the largest, moving slowly and all the time casting shifty glances at Jeff, as if he expected him to go back on his promise.

Jeff waited until Tex had dragged the three sacks into a pile before he backed away to their guns. He picked up both gunbelts then clutched them to his chest.

'I'm not so foolish as to think you won't still come after me even after I've let you have everything, so you're not getting your gun back and you ain't getting a horse.'

'How the hell am I supposed—?'

'Go back to Raw Creek and find a horse. Drag the money to Carmon. Bury it. I don't care what you do, but if you want the money, you'll find a way. And it'll take your mind off coming after me. But know this is: if I ever see you again, you're a dead man.'

Tex sat on the pile of sacks, a fortune he could now take nowhere, and contemplated him.

'But what will you ever find that's worth more than this?' he asked, his tone becoming resigned as he accepted his odd fate.

Jeff looked towards the arc of twilight on the horizon where Abigail then Todd and Samuel had gone, and the inhospitable and potentially lethal Barren Plains beyond.

'A life,' he said.

CHAPTER 9

When Jeff caught up with Todd and Samuel they had found Abigail. She was gesticulating at Todd, Jeff's arrival having interrupted a discussion.

Jeff jumped down from his horse and joined them.

'You all right?' Todd asked, eyeing Jeff's cut arm.

'I'll be fine,' Jeff said. 'Mike and me had ourselves a disagreement. We won't be riding together no more.'

'And what are the rest of us doing now?' Abigail asked, slapping her hands on her hips.

'I'll do what I promised Cassidy I'd do and keep everyone together and make sure you're all safe.'

'You can keep the rest safe. I'm going to the Barren Plains.'

'We're not splitting up.' Jeff looked at Todd, who nodded. 'And I reckon these two are as determined in that as I am.'

'You can't stop me leaving,' she snapped, stamping a foot. 'No matter how carefully you watch me, you'll have to sleep sometime.'

Jeff murmured an exasperated sigh, but Todd took advantage of the pause in the argument to edge forward.

'If I heard what you said right,' he said, looking at Jeff, 'you're not saying where we should go, just that we should stick together.'

'That's what I said,' Jeff said.

Todd stood tall and puffed his chest. 'Then I want to go to the Barren Plains and help Abigail find her sister.'

'I agree,' Jeff said, making Todd smile and Abigail nod with approval. Then he looked at Samuel, who shrugged and took several seconds to provide his sullen response.

'I ain't risking my life over somebody I don't know,' he murmured.

His comment made Todd sneer, but Jeff shrugged.

'In which case the majority decides. If you want to risk riding alone with nobody to look after you and feed you and water you and hold your hand, go back to Carmon. We're going into the Barren Plains.'

To add to the insult Jeff fetched Tex's gun and handed it over to Todd. Samuel's eyes flared with indignation and for a moment Jeff thought he would run for his horse and ride away, but then his shoulders sagged.

'Seems we're all going to die together, then,' he muttered.

'Where should we go first?' Abigail asked, looking at Jeff's map.

Jeff considered the sparse details provided for the Barren Plains, as he had often done, but he also considered something that was more important, his conscience. Last night before he'd slipped off to sleep he had resolved that he wouldn't lie again.

This was his first test of that resolution. He could try to feign greater knowledge than he had, but instead he hunched over the map. Aside from Bleak Point and the occasional landmarks there were five intriguing crosses. Four were small and dotted about the Barren Plains. A large one was in the centre at Bleak Point.

'To be honest I've never been there,' he said. 'All I know is what's on this map, but I reckon these crosses show old mine workings.'

'Why?'

Jeff smiled as she accepted his honest admittance without concern, then pointed out the various crosses.

'The silver mine has a big cross, so I assume it signifies the mine and the smaller ones represent disused workings.' He waited until she nodded encouragingly. 'And the one thing I know about prospectors is they follow tales about previous finds. So I reckon they could have gone here.'

Jeff pointed at the nearest cross, which was about eighty miles away.

'That's still a guess,' she said.

'It is, but we have no facts to help your quest and so anything we do is a guess. At least this gives us a destination.'

'All right, Patrick,' she said, giving him a warm smile for the first time since he'd disappointed her in Raw Creek.

Jeff took a deep breath. 'I prefer my friends to call me Jeff.'

Abigail's smile widened. 'All right, Jeff, and I'm sorry I doubted you before. I know you did what you did for a good reason and your change of mind means a lot to me.'

She waited for a response, but Jeff's mouth had gone dry and he couldn't find anything to say. So he settled for smiling then packed away the map.

With their destination decided, they began their trek into the Barren Plains.

The map didn't provide a definitive boundary for the area, but as they rode on through the day, the terrain became more stark and inhospitable. This didn't concern Jeff. He was doing something decent in which, despite the dangers ahead, for the first time in weeks he felt free.

His only anxious thought was why he hadn't had the courage to turn his back on the money earlier. Now that he had, he hoped that it wouldn't bring Tex any joy and he hoped that one day the law would find him and make him pay for having killed his alter-ego Patrick Carey.

Todd was also relaxed, clearly enjoying having had his opinion taken seriously, but their good moods didn't affect everyone. Samuel remained as surly as he had always been, and as the day wore on Abigail became withdrawn and morose. She didn't respond to Jeff's gentle probing about what was on her mind other than to provide short unhelpful answers.

At sundown they were over halfway to the cross and so when they set off early the next day, they hoped to reach their destination by sundown. The fresh day found her in better spirits.

'I'm sorry,' she said after they'd ridden along for an hour. 'I was quiet yesterday. I guess I've spent a long time battling to begin the search for my sister and with that battle over, I now have the time to think about the hopelessness of that mission.'

'I understand.'

'I know you do, and that's the other thing that's been worrying me.' She took a deep breath. 'You're not the man I thought you were.'

Jeff gulped. He had resolved not to lie again, but he had hoped he wouldn't have to deal with comments like this.

'In what way?'

'I'd heard about you in Carmon. Your reputation was poor, so I've changed my mind several times about why you've been nice to me, but I've decided there's nothing to worry about. It's simply that you're nothing like the Patrick Carey I'd heard about.'

Jeff breathed a sigh of relief. 'As I said to you yesterday: Patrick is a supplier. He seeks out profit, cuts costs, trims supplies. I'm Jeff, and Jeff is helping you find your sister.'

'I like Jeff more,' she said softly then made a swift turn to the front as if she'd said too much.

Her offhand comment resonated in Jeff's mind. If

it confirmed what he hoped it did, he deemed it worth more than the haul he'd left behind. But as the day wore on and they approached the place marked by the cross, other worries drove away the euphoria.

Although he had forced the danger they might encounter from his mind, he now had to face the fact that he hadn't freed himself from his past. Blake Kelly and the other men he'd double-crossed were in the Barren Plains and they could already be watching them. Even if they weren't, they had another pressing problem – water.

They had brought plenty, but their horses found little nourishment in the sparse vegetation and they had already used up a quarter of their supply. Unless they found water, they couldn't visit all the crosses and still get out of the area.

Not that he was even sure what the crosses represented. They were heading towards a prominent mound and from several miles away it appeared to be as smooth as an egg, with no sign of old mine workings.

When they reached the mound, Abigail expressed the same view.

'It's the only nearby landmark,' Jeff said, considering the outline of its perimeter on the map. 'The cross must mark something and there's only way to find out what that is. We'll go round it and see what we find.'

His positive outlook made her smile, but when they'd traipsed around the mound and seen nothing but smooth rock, they all became depressed.

'No workings,' Todd said, 'no sign of anyone coming here, no nothing.'

'Then why put a cross here?' Abigail said.

'Maybe the cross just notes that it's a prominent landmark.'

'There are other mounds and ridges and features out there and they're not marked with crosses.'

Todd shrugged then lowered his head as if he'd spoken too much. With nobody else offering a view everyone looked at Samuel, the only one to have crossed the plains before, but he shrugged in a vague manner that suggested he hadn't been listening.

'We can't give up,' Jeff said. 'We head on to the second cross and see what we can find there.'

He didn't say that if they found nothing their water would be getting low and they'd face a course of action Abigail wouldn't want to take, but his enthusiasm cheered her. So they set off for the second cross.

Late on the third day of travelling across the plains they caught their first sight of their new destination, and it was more promising. A craggy ridge of rock stood proudly on the plains, clearly providing more places where they could search than the mound.

As they approached it, Jeff looked for caves that might contain old workings, but couldn't see any. With the ridge being several miles long and the sun dipping to the horizon, they didn't have enough time for a proper search before it got dark. So they settled down against a sheer stretch of rock that protected them from the wind and when Todd had lit a fire, Jeff bade everyone to stay put while he had a brief scout around on foot.

He headed along the base of the ridge, peering up at the apex, but saw nothing worth investigating. By the time the sun had set he had walked for a half-mile and this new perspective let him see that the ridge had several deep gullies. Comparing these features to the map let him deduce that they had fortuitously camped at the spot where the cross had been marked.

Although the gathering darkness meant he wouldn't be able to search that night he felt more confident as he set off back to the camp. On the return journey he concentrated on the plains.

He saw nothing of interest, but when he entered the camp, the fire was providing a heartening glow and the enticing smell of a bubbling stew drifted to him. So without too much difficulty he made his report that he'd seen nothing sound optimistic.

Abigail nodded then gestured to him to sit while she filled his bowl. Jeff paced round to take a position beside the fire and as he bent to sit he casually glanced up at the ridge.

A man was looking down at them.

Jeff ducked and then with his head down he grabbed Abigail's arm and hurried into hiding against the rock wall. He judged that Todd and Samuel were sitting in a position that was out of the man's view, but he still beckoned for them to join him.

'What's wrong?' Abigail said.

'Someone's up there,' Jeff said, gesturing.

'Are you sure?' She considered his stern expression then looked up at the rock wall above them. 'Of course you are. What was he doing?'

Jeff thought back. He hadn't looked at the area above them much, so he didn't know how long the person had been standing there, but he'd chosen an obvious position and that implied confidence.

'There's only way to find out. Wait here.'

Jeff gave her an encouraging smile and then keeping close to the rock wall he edged along until he reached a point where he could climb the ridge. He judged that he was 200 yards to the side and a hundred feet below the position where the man had been standing. Unless the watcher was supremely arrogant he would have moved by now, but Jeff still scurried up the ridge with his head down.

When he was high enough to be level with the man, he sought a route to the side. He had to backtrack several times until he found a hollow that let him work his way along the ridge. He walked until he judged he was behind the camp.

On either side the terrain sloped away steeply. To his right was the top of the ridge and to his left was the unseen watcher. He headed to the left, clambering on hands and feet to reach him. With every step he expected to see his form appear ahead, but he reached the top without seeing him and the plains, now shrouded in advancing darkness appeared below.

Cautiously he slipped to the edge of the vertical rock, intent on locating where the watcher had been standing, and looked down. Abigail was below and she was pointing up, a hand held to her mouth. When she saw him, she gave an odd gesture of holding her hands together as if pleading.

Jeff stared down at her, wondering what the gesture meant then noticed that she was looking to his side. He swirled round and saw a gash in the rock thirty feet on.

Jeff's heart beat faster. The man could be there. In fact the gash was so thin he could have been there when they'd arrived and they wouldn't have seen him.

He edged along with his neck craned, aiming to see the danger ahead as early as possible, but when he saw what had shocked her, he realized what her gesture had meant and fell to his knees. She had been offering a prayer. He murmured a quick prayer himself then slipped into the indentation.

The standing man was still standing, but he had no choice. A stake held him upright, his hands tied behind him, his chin bound to the stake to keep his head raised. Although when he stood before him, he saw that the man had been unable to see the plains in his last moments. He had been blinded, his face so torn he was unrecognizable as the man he had been in life. Only the familiar trousers and boots, the only clothes he wore, let Jeff work out who he was: Tex Stroud.

Jeff stood as close to the edge as he dared and

considered his murderous partner of the last few weeks. He noted the signs of the lingering death Blake had carved into his bared chest. Then he cut him down.

The body was stiff, but Tex smelt no worse dead than alive so he judged that he'd died recently. It would have taken time to reach this place so it could even have happened earlier that day.

As the darkness would make it hard for him to find his footing, he postponed the decision as to whether to bury him.

'Hard to feel sorry for you, Tex,' he said, standing over the body. 'You enjoyed using that knife and in the end every cut you delivered got paid back to you tenfold.'

Then, with a shiver at the thought of what his punishment would be if Blake found him, he headed down to the camp. After he'd told Abigail who the dead man was, she asked the question that had been on his own mind.

'Why bring Mike all the way here to kill him?'

'I guess because Blake has taken refuge out here. . . .' He trailed off, unwilling to even hint of the shared history between Tex and Blake. 'The important thing is, he's gone.'

'How do you know that?'

'Because we're still alive.' Jeff went to the fire. He considered kicking it out, but he judged that it was guarded and not easily visible.

Then they settled down and with their backs to the rock wall they forced themselves to eat their meal.

The nourishment didn't cheer Jeff as he looked out at the darkened plains. Time passed slowly and as the cold descended each person shuffled down under a blanket.

Todd was sitting beside Samuel and so Jeff was pleased when Abigail sat beside him.

'Should we try to sleep?' she asked.

'Yeah. I'm sure we'll hear anyone approach.' What they would do then against men who could take Tex so easily he didn't know.

'How long had you known him?'

'Not long. What happened to him was bad, but I wouldn't describe us as being friends.'

'I noticed that you didn't see eye to eye.'

Jeff uttered a rueful laugh. 'Tex was an odd one and that's a fact.'

She swirled round to look at him with her brow knotted.

'Tex?'

Jeff shrugged beneath his blanket. 'Mike, if you prefer, although he's dead now so it doesn't matter none.'

She looked at the fire. 'You're Patrick, but you prefer your friends to call you Jeff and he was Tex but he preferred to be called Mike.'

Her tone was level and she didn't sound particularly concerned by this oddity, but even so after his resolution to avoid lying Jeff saw a potential line of questioning here that could get uncomfortable. And he found that he didn't have the energy to keep that resolution by avoiding the subject.

'Something like that,' he said, sounding distracted. 'I want us all to get some sleep, but I'll scout around first.'

He stood and gave her an encouraging pat on the shoulder, but she didn't reply, her failure to meet his eye suggesting she'd noted his abrupt change of subject. He'd made a mistake and feeling embarrassed he turned away before she sensed his discomfort.

He paced away taking the route he'd taken earlier and was relieved to see that their camp-fire became invisible after only a few dozen yards. When he reached the spot where he'd climbed the ridge, he stopped and sat on a rock to compose himself before returning.

'Will I ever be able to put my past behind me?' he said to himself.

He started to list the ways his attempt to move on could go wrong. There were many, but he didn't expect to get an answer.

'Never,' a voice said behind him.

At first he thought it had been his imagination, but then he heard a footfall and he accepted with a gulp that he hadn't been mistaken.

'Blake?' he asked.

'Who else?' The voice was gruff and came from ten feet behind him.

'Then take me and do your worst. I'm the only one responsible.'

Blake snorted a harsh laugh. 'That's what Tex said. It didn't help him none, and it won't help you.'

'Tex didn't deserve mercy, but the townsfolk of Raw Creek did.' Jeff stood, letting the motion move his jacket aside to free his gun. He would go for it when Blake came closer, but he knew there was little he could do against the vengeful wrath of Blake's Dark Riders. 'I didn't take you for a heartless killer. If I'd have known you were, I'd have let Cassidy's posse find you.'

'And I'm grateful you once helped me, but as for the townsfolk . . . they did only the same as I've been doing.'

Jeff waited for an explanation of Blake's cryptic comment, but when it didn't come he turned to face him. He was standing in the shadows, a few feet up the slope, looking down at him. In contravention of what he'd expected, he appeared to be alone.

'And what have you been doing?'

Blake sneered. 'Waiting to die.'

Blake took a step towards him, but then his feet collapsed beneath him and he tumbled down the slope to land in a sprawled heap at Jeff's feet.

'What's wrong?' Jeff murmured, backing away a pace in surprise.

Blake raised a hand, his eyes bright and pleading in the poor light.

'Help me,' he croaked.

CHAPTER 10

'He looks like he's been through hell,' Abigail said.

'He sure does,' Jeff murmured, still unsure of the situation after the unexpected turn of events. He'd dragged Blake to the camp, but after collapsing he had only muttered unintelligibly and not explained himself.

'Who is he?'

Jeff took a deep breath then lowered his voice.

'Don't tell Todd or Samuel, I don't want to worry them. It's Blake Kelly.'

Abigail recoiled, looking around with her eyes wide as if the rest of the Dark Riders would appear at any moment. Then she gestured at their two companions and bade them to stay where they were beside the rock.

'Why did you help him?' she asked.

'I couldn't leave him and besides I don't think he was behind the massacre at Raw Creek. Get him some water. That might revive him.'

'Food, not water,' Blake croaked raising himself. 'I

haven't eaten since I escaped from the Dark Riders.'

'You mean your men turned on you?'

Blake gave Jeff a rueful glare. 'No, my men were faithful, but when we reached the Barren Plains, the Dark Riders killed them. I fled here. Every time they returned I hid and they didn't find me, but I didn't dare to try to make it back across the plains.'

Jeff balked at the change in Blake's voice and attitude. Before, he'd been a confident man even when he'd fled from Cassidy, but not now.

'What did they want?'

'To make us suffer.'

Abigail arrived with a bowl of the scraps left over from their meal. They were cold and fatty, but Blake snatched the bowl from her grasp and wolfed down the scraps with his fingers.

'How long have you been here?' Jeff asked.

'Two weeks,' Blake said while chewing. 'A long time without food.'

'But not water?'

'There's a spring.' Blake pointed up the ridge. 'That's why the Dark Riders come here, and why we have to get away before they return.'

Jeff nodded then glanced at Abigail.

'The crosses don't indicate old mine workings,' he said.

'I heard,' she said. 'They mark something even more valuable than silver – water.'

'Which means,' he said, lowering his voice to a sympathetic tone, 'we're no closer to finding a place where a prospector would go.'

'I don't agree. Prospectors need water even more than everyone else does. So I'll still check out all the springs. If she's alive, she'd have had to find water and a spring is where she could be.'

While chewing, Blake jerked his head back and forth to watch their exchange. He licked the bowl then knelt.

'You have to leave,' he said in a stronger voice than before. 'Didn't you hear? The Dark Riders don't want anything but to make people suffer.'

Abigail looked at Jeff for his answer, but he stayed quiet, letting her speak.

'We stay,' she said simply.

'There's your decision, Blake,' Jeff said.

'You're both crazy,' Blake muttered, throwing the bowl to the ground, 'and soon to be screaming for mercy like Tex did.'

'How do you know his name?' Abigail asked.

Blake didn't reply immediately, letting Jeff butt in.

'I don't want to hear any more about Tex, but just so we're clear, Blake. I'm Patrick Carey. I work at the supply depot outside Monotony and I was taking supplies to Samuel's father at Bleak Point. I picked up Todd on the way and now I'm helping Abigail find her missing sister and husband. Nothing can stop me completing that task.'

His speech made Abigail cast an odd glance at him, but Jeff avoided catching her eye.

'That's interesting, *Patrick*,' Blake said, lowering his voice and spreading his hands in a gesture of acceptance.

His movement and change in tone alerted Jeff, so when Blake leapt to his feet and swung a fist at his face, he was ready. He jerked backwards, avoiding the blow, but Blake followed through by barging into him. They went down with Blake landing on top of him and clawing at his face.

Jeff braced himself then pushed Blake away, making him roll. Blake came to a halt on his back, wheezing as he caught his breath then slowly got to his feet.

'You're too weak to fight,' Jeff said.

'I'm not,' Blake grunted. 'I'll make you pay.'

Blake came at him with his fists raised, but Jeff paced aside and let him run on by. Then he helped him on his way with a kick to the rump that sent him ploughing into the dirt. Blake slapped his hands to the ground and tried to lift himself but then flopped down.

'You'll make nobody pay,' Jeff said, 'and if you attack me again, I'll leave you here for the Dark Riders to find.'

Blake raised his head, fear making his eyes shine in the firelight.

'What do I have to say to make you leave?'

'Nothing. We're searching for someone. We won't leave until we find her.'

Blake shuffled round to a sitting position and provided a weak and forlorn shrug.

'Then what if I take you to her?' he said casually. 'Would that let you leave?'

'You don't—'

'Where?' Abigail screeched, setting off towards Blake.

'Don't answer that,' Jeff muttered to Blake. He grabbed her arm as she passed and pulled her away from Blake. 'He just said that to torment you. He knows nothing.'

'I know that,' she said, her pained tone and wide eyes suggesting that in her mind hope was still defeating common sense. 'But I still want to hear what he has to say.'

'A huge rock monolith,' Blake said, unconcerned by their disagreement. He held up two fingers to demonstrate. 'Like two fingers jutting into the air. That's all I'm saying.'

Blake's expression was serious, so Jeff released Abigail's arm then drew out his map and laid it on the ground before him. Jeff pointed out their current location then stood back, still expecting deception.

Blake peered at the map, moved it around until he had an angle he liked, then pointed.

Jeff looked down to see that he'd pinpointed one of the crosses they'd yet to visit.

'Then that is where we'll go,' he said.

When Jeff first saw their destination, he accepted that the description was accurate.

A great rock monolith sprouted out from the plains. Scree skirted around it up to a point where the stone had split down the middle to create two towers, one having fallen away to stand precariously as if the finger would press down at any moment.

Throughout the day Blake had led while Samuel and Todd had ridden doubled-up. Jeff had expected that Blake would bolt, even though he was unlikely to survive without water, but he'd ridden on.

So when they stopped at the base of the scree Jeff waited for Abigail to ask the question Blake couldn't delay answering any longer. Abigail merely looked at him with her eyebrows raised and in response Blake gestured at the gap between the rock towers, then raised two fingers and pointed at the webbing of his fingers signifying where they should go.

Unwilling to let Blake out of his sight, Jeff ordered him to lead and with a shrug, Blake set off. Jeff told Todd and Samuel to stay at the base while he and Abigail followed Blake.

There was no sign of life or of the promised spring. So, as they climbed, Abigail looked at Jeff, her expression tense as she presumably awaited for Blake to play out whatever cruel deception he had planned.

With stones falling away when they stood on them and turning most of their upwards steps into downward slides they had to fight to climb every pace. So when they reached the top of the scree Abigail and Jeff were clutching hold of each other and taking it in turns to stop the other falling, while Blake fought his own way on ahead.

Blake reached the gap between the rocks first and disappeared from view. Deciding that Blake would make a bolt for freedom Jeff hurried on, pulling

Abigail up the last few yards, but when he reached the thin stretch of flat rock beyond, Blake had stopped a few paces on. He was pointing to the base of one tower.

Jeff peered around his body then winced and turned to Abigail, aiming to bid her to remain there, but she shot him a warning glare then hurried past him and Blake. Her step faltered when she saw what was ahead. Then she shuffled to the spot that Blake had indicated. She knelt down and lowered her head.

Jeff moved on to stand beside Blake, although he kept him in view in case he took the opportunity to run, but he stood as sombrely as Jeff did while Abigail considered the grisly find.

Bones were all that remained. Scavengers had scattered them but Jeff judged that they were human and that more than one person was here, although perhaps not the four people who had been mentioned in the story Abigail had been told. She rooted around, but found no clothing or belongings.

'How do you know whose they are?' she asked, looking up.

'You're risking my life with every moment you stay here,' Blake said, setting his feet wide apart and folding his arms in a gesture of defiance. 'So I'm saying nothing until the Barren Plains is behind me.'

Jeff considered Blake's confident stance then Abigail's pleading expression that said she both wanted to believe her sister was still alive while wanting the relief of an end to her quest.

'He knows nothing, Abigail,' Jeff said. 'All we know for sure is someone died here. The search goes on.'

'It does not!' Blake snapped. 'I've completed my promise. Now complete your promise, *Patrick*.'

Blake's emphasis left Jeff in no doubt as to what he would say next if he didn't give in to his demand. Jeff wrestled with his dilemma and he was no nearer to a solution when Samuel shouted out from behind him.

'Come quickly,' he said between gasps. 'It's Cassidy.'

Jeff turned to see Samuel clamber over the edge. He was red-faced and panting after exerting himself for the first time since they'd left the depot. Abigail hurried over to join him and looked down at the plains.

'He's right,' she said. 'It's the convoy. They must have followed us.'

She put a hand to her brow and took a few paces down the slope while waving but Jeff didn't need to see proof. Instead, he joined Blake.

'You'll never get to leave now,' Jeff said.

'If Cassidy recognizes me, I won't,' Blake whispered. 'If he doesn't, keep the woman quiet about my identity, or I'll make sure you're in as much trouble as I am.'

'And if I help you?'

'I'll tell you how I know that's her sister's body.'

Jeff considered the offer then leaned towards Blake.

'Accepted.' He waited until Blake nodded before

continuing, 'With one change. Tell me what you know, then I'll get you out of this.'

Cassidy jumped down from the lead wagon at the base of the monolith and received a breathless summary of the last few days' exploits from Todd. Then he bade him to stand back while he waited for the others to join him.

Abigail and Samuel stayed at the top of the monolith, presumably so that she could search for whatever she had been led here to see, but the other two men came down the slope. Even before they had reached the bottom Cassidy had confirmed his suspicion but he kept his expression welcoming as he greeted each man then waited to hear their version of events.

As it turned out, Patrick Carey spoke up and provided him with the same tale as Todd had. So Cassidy paced back and forth, ruminating.

'So,' he said finally, 'you've had a harrowing last few days?'

'Sure,' Patrick said. 'And you?'

'Sure.'

Cassidy reckoned he didn't need to relate what had happened.

He had found the burnt-out remnants of the previous convoy that hadn't made it through to Bleak Point. The supplies had gone but the bodies hadn't. Those that hadn't been shot in the assault had been staked out and tortured.

So Cassidy had been cautious and had holed up at

a large mound where he'd discussed with the others whether they should continue. But the debate had been curtailed when they'd found recent tracks. They'd followed them and found Mike's body and now the others.

'Are you staying with us?' Patrick waited for an answer, but as Cassidy was avoiding giving him any clues as to his state of mind he kept quiet. 'Because we intend to continue searching for Abigail's sister and that won't take us to Bleak Point for a while.'

'And will your quiet new companion stay with you?' Cassidy turned to this man and received a nod.

'He doesn't speak much,' Patrick said, 'but he led us here and he has other places to take us.'

'Has he?' Cassidy took a slow pace backwards, his odd actions making the two men glance at each other. 'Final chance, Patrick.'

'Final chance for what?' Patrick murmured, although a catch in his voice suggested he was getting an inkling that all was not well.

Cassidy went to the wagon and gestured to the two men sitting on the seat. Despite his initial misgivings he had come to trust and rely upon the men Patrick had hired and accordingly with quiet efficiency the men jumped down and paced over to stand around Patrick and his companion. Then, while keeping an eye on them, Cassidy removed a half-filled sack from the back of the wagon and threw it to Patrick's feet.

'You know. Tell me what's in the sack and I'll listen. Say nothing and I won't.'

Patrick glanced at the sack. 'I have no idea. It's not

one of mine.'

The sack wasn't his, but Cassidy could tell from Patrick's shifty glances at it that he had a good idea what was inside.

'That was your final chance. You are now under arrest.'

'Why?' Patrick bleated while his companion glanced at the two men standing beside them, then at the plains, presumably looking for somewhere to run to even though the attempt would be futile.

'You found Mike's body, but you didn't search the area. I did. I'm guessing his killers stole what he had on him, but left what they didn't deem valuable. That's what's in the sack. Bonds, deeds, stocks . . . and they all bear the name of people from Carmon, the place where he stole them.'

Patrick gulped. 'I don't know nothing about that.'

'As I said, I was prepared to listen. All I needed was the name of your companion, but now I'll have to name him myself.' Cassidy turned to that man. 'Howdy, Blake Kelly. I've waited a while to catch up with you.'

While Patrick opened and closed his mouth trying to appear shocked, Blake had the grace to hold out his hands in a gesture of surrender.

Cassidy gestured for the two men to secure his prisoners. Blake didn't resist, but Patrick threw the hand that descended on his shoulder away.

'Wait!' he said. 'This ain't like it seems.'

'I don't care,' Cassidy said. 'The time for explanations is over.'

'But there's—'

A scream tore out from the monolith then echoed between the two towers of rock. Down on the ground everyone froze, staring up at the rock, but nobody came into view. Patrick was the first to move when he barged the man attempting to arrest him aside. Then he ran for the slope.

Cassidy ordered everyone to stay with the wagons and look after Blake then ran after him. Patrick was several paces ahead of him, letting him keep an eye on him, but he didn't expect trouble. No matter what his involvement with Blake had been he accepted that his concern was genuine.

No further cries of alarm sounded as they climbed, but as they closed on the top Patrick tired, his plodding paces digging deep holes in the loose rocks. Cassidy passed him to reach the top first. He hadn't known what to expect but the sight that greeted him shocked him into stopping, letting Patrick catch up with him.

Patrick grunted in anger and moved to push by him, but Cassidy held him back.

'I'll deal with it,' he muttered then hurried off.

On the other side of the flat length of rock Abigail was on her back and struggling to fight off Samuel. Both her hands were locked in his as he bore down on her, trying to pin her down.

In four long paces Cassidy reached them then yanked Samuel off her. He noted her disarrayed clothing and when he swung Samuel round, his cheeks were flushed and the left one sported a series of bloody scratches.

'I weren't doing nothing,' Samuel murmured, fighting his way out of Cassidy's grip.

Abigail screeched out a denial then hurried away to Patrick, who wrapped his arms around her and held her head to his chest while glaring murderously over her shoulder at Samuel.

'You were,' Cassidy said. 'Explain yourself.'

'It was her!' he yelled, then pointed at Abigail while wiping his raked cheeks with his other hand. He flinched then removed his hand and looked at the bloody fingertips, apparently noticing his injury for the first time. The sight made him flare his eyes. 'She's been making eyes at me ever since we left Carmon.'

'She hasn't.' Cassidy stabbed a firm finger against Samuel's chest that made him back away for a pace. He punctuated each of his points with another stab of the finger that made Samuel take another pace backwards. 'Your pa thought this trip would make a man of you. He thought you'd learn some responsibility. And I thought you'd do some work instead of idling away your days, except it seems the only thing on your mind was ogling Abigail.'

'And yours,' Samuel murmured sulkily.

'You're wrong, you worthless piece of trash.'

'You can't speak to me like that.'

Blood roared in Cassidy's ears. His vision contracted until all he could see was Samuel's arrogant sneer.

'Then maybe I should speak to you in a way you

will understand.'

Cassidy swung back his fist and put his frustrations over Samuel's repeated failures into a haymaker of punch to the jaw.

Samuel went spinning away. Then he disappeared.

The disappearance was so unexpected that Cassidy had to shake himself and then jerk back a pace as he struggled to understand what had happened. He looked down to see that while he'd been annoyed and pushing Samuel backwards they'd backed away to stand on the edge of the flat rock. Samuel had fallen over the side.

He moved forward as a scream sounded, the sound getting further away faster than he expected. The area ahead opened up and, unlike the other side of the monolith, he couldn't see any cushioning scree.

A thud sounded, far below. The screaming stopped.

With mounting trepidation Cassidy leaned forward. The ground 300 feet below appeared and there was no sign of broken and weathered rocks. It was a sheer drop. And at the bottom of that drop lay the broken form of Samuel, his limbs twisted into shapes they would never naturally adopt and making him hope for his sake that he was dead.

He still hurried past Patrick and Abigail then back down the scree to ground level. But when he'd ran round the two-fingered rock to reach the body, he [illegible]nd that he had been right.

[illegible]moment of anger he had killed a good [illegible]son.

*

'I don't blame you, Cassidy,' Jeff said. 'If you hadn't have killed him, I would have.'

'Coming from you,' Cassidy said, 'that don't give me no comfort.'

Jeff shrugged as much as the bonds that tied him to the wagon wheel would allow. Blake was tied to the other wheel with crossed ropes, but perhaps in recognition of Jeff's less dangerous status, Cassidy had used only a single rope to secure him.

'I'll let that insult pass, but only because you know I'm not like that, otherwise you'd never risk taking me to Bleak Point.'

Cassidy narrowed his eyes. 'What does that mean?'

'It means I've just seen you kill Frank Holmes's son, but your friend might not want to hear the truth about what happened and even if he does, you might not want to tell it to him.'

Cassidy nodded slowly then leaned down to glare at Jeff.

'So your threat is: if I don't release you, you'll make things hard for me and Frank?'

'I didn't say that. I know you're a decent man. I know you'll tell him a story that'll present a more acceptable version of events, and you'll do that to spare his pain and not to save yourself.'

'So what are you saying?'

'That I'm not blackmailing you. The man you think I am would do that, but I won't.'

Cassidy acknowledged this statement by making

his stance less belligerent and stepping back for a pace.

'Obliged for that,' he said in a softer tone, 'but that still doesn't change what you did and what I have to do about it.'

'I know, but it should. I made an understandable mistake. So did you. Neither of us should pay for that mistake for the rest of our lives.'

Cassidy snorted. 'You can't claim my mistake was anything like yours.'

'I can't. Yours was worse. I made a mistake because I was hungry. You were angry and killed a defenceless young man.'

Cassidy opened his mouth to snap back a response, but then he slapped a fist against his thigh, turned on his heel and left him, leaving Jeff with only Blake for company. Accordingly, Blake shot him a glare that appeared to blame him for his present predicament before he too turned away.

With the camp and rock being on the opposite side of the wagons Jeff stared at the plains. The only feature was the distant spire of Bleak Point, still appearing no closer than it had been at Raw Creek. Idly he considered his last conversation with Blake wondering whether Abigail would want to hear what he had learnt now that the truth about his identity had emerged.

At sundown he was no nearer to a solution, but he was pleased that Abigail brought him his meal. Cassidy fed Blake while another man stayed back and cast cautious glances at everyone.

'Cassidy said you're not dangerous,' she said with her head bowed, 'so I'll spoon it in.'

Her failure to meet his eye resolved Jeff's dilemma. He would tell her, but later when she might not feel so aggrieved about him.

'He's right. I'm not dangerous, and please don't hate me.'

'I don't,' she said, looking up at him. 'With the shock of what Samuel tried to do and the worry about those bones, I'm just too numb to think about who you really are.'

'I'm Jeff Steed, a decent man. I made a mistake when I was hungry and accepted a job for twenty dollars from—'

'Twenty dollars! Cassidy said it was for thousands.'

Jeff sighed. Then slowly at first in case she didn't want to hear him out he told her what he'd done for the last few weeks. She knelt to listen and whenever he paused she spooned in a mouthful. Jeff swallowed and continued, leaving nothing out, even his greed and details that put his role in a bad light. She didn't speed up her feeding so he presumed his tale wasn't unwelcome.

'And that,' he said finishing off, 'is how I got here. I lied, but there's one thing I never lied about – that I wanted to help you, and that I care about you.'

She considered his empty plate then opened her mouth to respond, but then closed it. With whatever was on her mind left unsaid she left him.

He watched her leave until she disappeared with Cassidy around the end of the wagon, then sighed and leaned back to look up at the twilight sky.

Blake uttered a sneering chuckle.

'What a heart-warming speech,' he said in a mocking tone. ' "I care about you!" I can tell you, she don't care about you no more.'

'Be quiet. I gave her plenty to think about. Maybe before we part company she'll forgive me.'

'Part company! What an idiotic way of saying getting ripped to pieces by the Dark Riders.'

'Cassidy has plenty of help. If they find us and attack, he'll see them off.'

'They will find us and they will attack.' Blake looked at the plains, now glowing red in the last rays of sunlight. 'And it'll be soon.'

'How can you know that?'

Blake let out a long sigh then spoke up with a slow and funereal tone.

'They're not called the Dark Riders because they wear dark clothes.' He looked at Jeff and his tone couldn't disguise the fear in his eyes. 'It's because they come when it's dark.'

CHAPTER 11

'Cassidy!' Jeff called out again.

'He ain't coming,' Blake said. 'Be quiet.'

'Abigail!' Jeff called. 'I need to talk to you. Everybody's life depends on it. The Dark Riders are coming.'

'They ain't listening, but the Dark Riders are. They're out there waiting to—'

'Be quiet.' Jeff moved as far forward as his bonds would let him and turned. He'd been tethered to a single spoke. If he were to kick the wood repeatedly, he might be able to break through. He laughed. 'I can escape if I have to. You can't. If the Dark Riders come, you'll be tied up and unable to stop them giving you what Tex got.'

This taunt had the desired effect and made Blake quieten then look away to peer into the darkness, leaving Jeff to continue calling out for someone to come.

He hoped he'd attract Abigail, but when someone did arrive, he was surprised to see that it was Todd.

He shuffled towards him, then with a stomp of his bare feet he stopped ten feet away, making it clear he wouldn't risk coming any closer.

'Shut up,' he said. 'We want to sleep.'

'You can't. The Dark Riders are out there.'

'We heard you and even without the warning, Cassidy has taken steps to protect us.'

'Then I wish him luck.' Jeff considered Todd's uncertain stance. 'But is there some other reason why you came to tell me that?'

Todd pouted, looking as if he wouldn't answer, then shook a fist.

'I looked up to you. I thought you were Patrick Carey. I thought I'd proved myself and you'd give me a permanent job, but you lied to me.'

Jeff fixed Todd with his gaze. 'If it helps, if I were Patrick Carey, I'd employ you, but you never had to prove yourself to me, only yourself. Now you've done that, you'll have the confidence to get a proper job.'

Todd frowned and lowered his head, perhaps showing that despite Jeff having disappointed him, he still wanted his approval.

'I will,' he snapped, turning away. 'And I sure won't make the same mistakes as you did.'

'Then it was all worth it. And Todd.' Jeff waited until he stopped. 'If they come, look after yourself.'

Todd muttered something to himself then disappeared from view beyond the side of the wagon.

'Will you now end your incessant whimpering?' Blake asked, from the other wheel. 'Because I'd sooner get torn to pieces by the Dark Riders than listen to you whining on to every person in the convoy.'

Jeff started to snap back a retort, but then saw movement in the darkness.

'You might get that wish sooner than you feared,' he said.

Blake swung round to look in the same direction as Jeff was, narrowing his eyes as he peered at the nothingness beyond the wagons. Then the movement came again, a low shape moving close to the ground and towards them. With his eyes now being attuned to what to look out for, Jeff saw more forms behind this one. And they were closing on the wagons.

He glanced at Blake and in unison they yelled for help.

'It's the Dark Riders!' Blake cried.

'They're here!' Jeff shouted.

Cassidy had ignored every other warning, but Jeff reckoned he couldn't ignore this one, especially as Blake was now screeching at the top of his voice. Then one of the approaching forms raised itself and a flash of light flew at Blake. It turned over in the air, letting Jeff see what it was a moment before the knife thudded into Blake's chest, making him cry out.

As Blake slumped, Jeff dropped to the ground to lie flat, the action saving him from a second knife, which flew over his shoulder and skidded on beyond the wagon. In desperation Jeff did the only thing he could do and wormed his way beneath the wagon seeking the inadequate cover of the wheel.

He peered through the spokes to see that the shapes were closer. He counted five forms in a line with another five further back in the shadows.

Jeff prepared himself to shout out another warning, accepting that even with the small profile he was presenting it would be the last thing he did, but then Cassidy shouted out orders from behind him and footfalls pounded. The wagon creaked as somebody clambered on top of it and the first defensive shot echoed from above him.

With the element of surprise lost, as one the Dark Riders raised themselves and ran for the wagons. Jeff watched them approach, firing as they ran. His inability to help the convoy or defend himself made him feel wretched, but he breathed a sigh of relief when they veered away then ran on until they were out of sight.

As gunfire tore out from numerous directions, Jeff kicked the wheel, but it was more solid than he'd feared. Then he looked around for the knife that had been thrown at him. He saw it gleaming beyond the wagon twenty yards away and out of his reach.

So he looked at Blake, lying slumped against his wheel, and at the knife protruding from his chest. Experimentally Jeff tugged at his rope and found that it gave him several feet of leeway, but perhaps not enough to reach the knife.

He tried it anyhow.

On his knees with his bound hands thrust out before him, Jeff worked his way towards the other wheel. From out of his view repeated cracks of gunfire were sounding. The impossibility of working out how well the defenders were doing added fevered desperation to his progress.

Jeff jerked to a sudden halt. He was four feet from the wheel. He slipped on to his side then squirmed to ensure the rope wasn't constrained and that let him move forward another two feet, but he was still some distance from the knife. His head was beside Blake's leg and he judged that if he could raise himself then move forward, he might be able to grab the knife in his teeth.

He strained, but the rope that tied him to the wheel was already taut. He strained again, a grunt escaping his lips, and to his surprise this made Blake's eyes roll down to consider him.

'You're alive,' Jeff murmured.

'Yeah,' Blake murmured. He glanced at the knife then shook himself, the action moving the blade and opening the wound. Blood spurted.

'Blake, know this: I'm sorry I double-crossed you and I never wanted it to end this way.'

Blake snorted. A bubble of blood dribbled from his lips.

'My only regret is not being able to stick you with this knife.'

He thrust out his chest, again making the knife shake, then gritted his teeth as a spasm of pain tore through him. Jeff also grunted when Blake's bound legs flailed against his head, but his eyes remained fixed on the knife as it rose then fell, willing Blake's squirming to work it loose.

'A nice end,' Blake murmured from above him, his voice like the wind, 'watching you squirming beneath me while I. . . .'

Blake's voice became too weak to hear his statement. Then he let out a rasping sigh. His body fell to the side to dangle suspended from the bonds that tied him. His mouth fell open, his eyes unfocused. He gave a final twitch.

Then the knife slipped from his chest to land on the ground.

Jeff looked at the knife, lying feet from his face, then wormed his way round to lie beneath Blake's body. He looked up at his face, getting so close that the blood dripping from Blake's chest splattered his hair.

'Just a few more inches,' Jeff murmured to himself then dug in his heels and strained to drag himself on and reach the knife.

His struggling must have stretched the rope because inch by inch he dragged himself closer until the knife was before his eyes. He opened his mouth then swooped for the knife, but a foot clamped down on the blade, pinning it to the ground and a hand slapped down on it then raised it from his view.

Jeff groaned with disappointment then looked up, but it was to see Todd's eager young face. Todd winked then knelt and rolled him on to his side. A few sawing motions cut through his bonds and then Jeff was free and sitting up.

'Obliged you helped me,' he said.

'Don't think I've forgiven you,' Todd said. 'I just

reckon Cassidy needs every man he can get.'

Jeff patted Todd's shoulder. 'I reckon he's got the best one here.'

Despite his earlier comment, this compliment made Todd smile. Then he pulled Jeff to his feet.

Jeff took the knife and used it to free himself from the last coils of rope. Then he stretched and looked around. Nobody was on this side of the wagons so he couldn't tell how the assault was progressing.

He started to ask Todd for a report, but Todd shook his head then beckoned for him to follow. He did as he'd been told and hurried after Todd down the gap between the wagons. When he came out on the other side he saw that the convoy members had been pinned down on that side.

Cassidy and the rest of the men were strung out along the side and beneath the final wagon and venturing out to trade gunfire with the Dark Riders, who had gone to ground behind a sprawling collection of boulders.

Abigail was kneeling in a recess in the supplies on the second wagon. Although she was protected from the sides and behind she was clutching a rifle. She started to swing it towards them then saw who was coming. To Jeff's relief she smiled then beckoned for him to join her.

'I can't,' Jeff said. 'I have to help Cassidy. Stay there.'

'Then be careful,' she said.

Jeff nodded then looked at Todd aiming to suggest he kept out of danger with her, but the determined look Todd gave him made him keep quiet. Then with his back to the wagon he and Todd made their way along to Cassidy, who was leaning over the end of the wagon and firing at the boulders.

Cassidy jerked back into hiding to let the next man take over. While he was reloading he turned and saw them. With his gaze set on Jeff, Cassidy spoke briefly with one man, clearly issuing orders, then slapped his shoulder and moved over to meet them.

He looked Jeff up and down, appraising his free state.

'Your gun's over there,' he said without preamble, then pointed at the blankets piled around the abandoned fire. 'If you can reach it, I'd welcome your help.'

Jeff nodded. He waited until Cassidy laid down a burst of covering fire at the boulders then ran for his gun.

He skidded to a halt on his side and slapped a hand on the cold metal then turned, planning to run back into hiding, but from his new position he could see all three wagons. And several Dark Riders were creeping along the tops of the wagons.

He glanced at Cassidy's position, seeing that he and the rest of his men were looking at the boulders where they presumed all the attackers were in hiding.

'They're coming over the wagons!' Jeff shouted, pointing.

His comment made Cassidy turn and look up at the tops of the wagons, but from his position he couldn't see the approaching men.

Then the main bulk of the Dark Riders jumped up from behind the boulders and laid down a burst of determined gunfire that tore into the side of the wagon. This made the defenders cringe back out of sight or dive to the ground.

Jeff also dived to the ground, but he hadn't been their target. As he got back to his feet he saw that the gunfire had been the cue for the men on the wagons to speed their approach. He broke into a run.

In the recess in the supplies Abigail was looking around as she tried to work out where the attackers were. Then she flinched and looked towards the nearest man. This man was out of her sight, but he was just feet away from her on the other side of a crate.

She placed her back to one side of the recess and aimed her rifle at the spot where the man would come into her view, but Jeff removed that potential battle when on the run he fired at the man. His first bullet slammed into the man's shoulder making him roll away and his second caught him in the chest making him flop.

Then, with the element of surprise gone, the rest of the attackers leapt to their feet.

Jeff threw himself to the side to save himself from a volley of gunshots that tore into the ground by his feet. He rolled then came up running towards the wheel, several feet to Abigail's side. Another slug tore down at him, so close it felt as if a gnat had bitten his cheek, before he reached cover beneath the wagon.

From there, he took stock of the situation.

Cassidy and his group had now seen the approaching men and had adopted the same posture as he had, sitting on their haunches under the cover of the end wagon while peering up, awaiting their assault.

Out of his sight gunfire sounded, close to and coming from above him. It was directed at Cassidy's men and thankfully it didn't find a target, but with them now being pinned down and defending themselves from two directions, that luck wouldn't hold out for long.

Jeff worked his way under the wagon until he judged he was beneath Abigail's position. He swung himself up to a standing position, the motion moving him into the path of a rifle barrel. He stared down the barrel then breathed a sigh of relief when he saw that Abigail was at the other end. She gave him a long look then jerked it aside, letting him vault up on to the wagon to join her.

'You're lucky I didn't kill you,' she said.

'Make sure the next one isn't so lucky,' Jeff said, then darted up to see where the Dark Riders were. At least two men were on each wagon and they were all looking at Cassidy's position, but both the men on their wagon saw him before he ducked from view.

Jeff prepared himself to leap out and confront them before they got a chance to sneak up on the recess. He glanced at Abigail aiming to tell her to stay down, but the determined look in her eyes said she'd ignore him.

Then he jumped up onto the pile of sacks to his

side, keeping his profile low. With his gun thrust out before him he picked out the man ahead of him and fired. His slug ripped into the man's side and made him fall from the wagon.

Then Jeff rolled on to his side, aiming to pick out the second man, but he wasn't in the position he had been in before. He got to his knees and looked for him, then felt the sacks he was kneeling on shift position a moment before a solid weight slammed into his back.

He went down, his chest crushed to the sack beneath him, the man straddling him and pinning him down. Cold metal pressed against the back of his neck and ground in.

With just moments before his assailant fired he tried to buck him away, but gunfire roared. He continued to squirm, feeling amazed he was still alive and not knowing how the man could have missed. The weight fell away from him. He twisted round to see the man on his knees and pitching forward, a smoking hole in his back.

Behind the falling body, Abigail stood, the rifle held to her shoulder, her back braced against the crate behind her.

Jeff started to thank her, but then her gaze swung round to a point behind him. She levered the rifle then fired over his shoulder. A thud sounded behind him as a man that Jeff hadn't seen fell. Then she was on her knees, flexing her shoulder and reloading.

Jeff threw himself on his chest then checked on who else was on the wagons, this time more carefully than before.

Cassidy had taken care of the men on the lead wagon, they had cleared the middle wagon, and only two men were on the endmost one. He levelled his gun on the nearest of those men and fired. The slug tore into a sack a foot to the man's side as did his second shot.

Before he could fire again the man swung round, his action alerting the second man and in unison they faced Jeff. Both their guns sighted him. Jeff took steadier aim and fired at the same time as they did.

One of their slugs tore into the sack beneath him, spraying corn into his face. The second skittered past his shoulder, but his shot hit the man on the left squarely between the eyes.

Then Jeff had to reload.

He rolled on to his back, trying to squirm down between two sacks to gather whatever cover they could provide while punching in bullets with fevered haste. Gunfire cracked from several directions, but Jeff put that from his mind and concentrated on his task.

Then with a spin of the barrel he rolled on to his front and planted his elbows squarely, but he was greeted with the sight of his target on his knees and turned away from him, clutching a bloodied shoulder. Abigail wasn't visible and Jeff couldn't tell who had shot him, but he stayed his own hand, unable to shoot this man in the back.

Then the man righted himself and started to turn but before Jeff could fire, a second slug tore into him and sent him tumbling from the wagon.

This time Jeff saw who had fired. Todd was standing in clear space, his gun aimed at the man, his mouth open in shock, presumably from having been forced to shoot a man for the first time.

Jeff gestured at him then at the wagon, urging him to get into cover, but Todd only looked towards him, his mouth still open.

'Get down,' Jeff shouted.

'No, you!' Todd shouted, his hand rising to point at him.

Jeff stared at him, wondering what his order had meant, then realized he was pointing past him. He swung round on his belly and found himself facing the man Abigail had shot a few moments earlier. His left arm was bloodied and dangling uselessly as he loomed over him, his gun swinging round to aim down at him.

With only a moment to react Jeff kicked out. His foot slammed into the man's knee as he fired, veering his aim and wasting the bullet into the sacks. The man toppled, but he fell on top of Jeff, an unfortunately placed elbow slamming into Jeff's stomach and blasting all the air from his chest.

Temporarily losing his breath, Jeff floundered. The man pinned him down, but with the sack he was lying on being at an angle, they slipped then toppled to the side. They rolled over each other coming to rest a few feet down the side of the bulging cargo with Jeff lying on his back.

One-handed the man brought his gun round. Jeff

tried to match the action, but then found that he had lost his own gun when he'd fallen. Frantically he searched around for it, but he couldn't find it as the man rocked his gun down to aim at his chest. From so close he couldn't miss and as they had fallen into a hollow he would get no help.

Jeff still reached around for the missing gun and his questing hand landed on a solid object. His heart thudded with hope, but with no time to check he'd been right, he ripped the object up towards the man's chest.

Only as it hit home did he see that he hadn't been mistaken, but by then it was too late for his assailant. The knife he'd used to free himself was buried to the hilt in the man's chest.

The man jerked backwards, his gun falling from his slack fingers as his useless hand clawed at the knife. Then he toppled over before rolling away to the ground.

Jeff breathed a sigh of relief then cautiously crawled up to the apex of the sacks. He reclaimed his gun on the way and when he peered over the top he saw that none of the Dark Riders was left on the wagons. A quick glance around confirmed nobody else was sneaking up on them.

They had defeated a major part of the attackers' forces.

With just the group that was pinning Cassidy down at one end of the wagons to defeat, for the first time Jeff reckoned they might survive the attack. When he joined Abigail in the recess, he reported as such.

'No matter how well we're doing,' she said, 'don't tell me to stay here until this is over.'

'Please do,' Jeff said.

'Why?'

'Because I don't want anything to happen to you.' He gripped her arms tightly then pushed her gently into a corner of the recess. Then he moved to leave, aiming to help Cassidy, but she grabbed his arm.

'But it's the same for me.'

He patted her hand. 'Something will always happen to me. I did wrong, so even if I survive this I'll go to jail. When I'm there I need to know you're fine, even if we can never be together.'

She started to say something, but a fierce burst of gunfire silenced her.

Down on the ground Todd flinched and hurried into hiding with his back pressed against the wagon. Jeff beckoned for him to join them. Todd stood for a moment, but when a second prolonged burst of gunfire tore out, he jumped on to the wagon.

Jeff gave Todd a pat on the back and Abigail an encouraging smile, to which she responded with a pleading look that asked him not to go. Despite that, he jumped down.

Cassidy's group didn't appear to have lost anyone and they were spread out keeping low and facing the boulders. With the defenders having found the best positions to keep themselves safe, he looked around for a place to lie where he could make a difference.

A slug whined close by and out of the corner of his eye Jeff saw wood splinter from the side of the wagon.

It could have been an unfortunate ricochet, but then he saw a sack kick and split, then another. He swirled round to face the fire and with a gulp he realized what must have happened.

One of the Dark Riders had slipped around to this side of the wagon and was firing at them from a hidden position.

Todd and Abigail were looking in the same direction as he was and without him asking them to move, they jumped down from the wagon aiming to get into hiding. Jeff shouted out a warning to Cassidy, making Cassidy turn, but he was too late.

One of his men spun away clutching his chest.

Then a cry sounded from closer to and in frozen horror Jeff saw Todd go down. He fell against Abigail who grabbed hold of him. She tried to right him, but he bent over and she had no choice but to drag him under the wagon and behind a wheel.

Jeff joined her. 'How is. . . ?'

He trailed off when he saw Todd had been shot in the neck and he could manage only strangulated gasps. Jeff met her eyes as she cradled him and gave her a brief shake of the head.

'Where is that damn shooter?' she said, looking through the wheel at the darkness beyond.

Jeff was thinking the same thing as another burst of gunfire tore along the wagons. By now Cassidy's men had gone to ground and were keeping themselves protected from this new source of trouble as best as they were able. But with gunfire raining down on them from two directions, they were in trouble if they couldn't locate the new assailant.

Another burst of gunfire tore along the wagons making Jeff realize the problem was worse than he'd first thought.

'It's shooters,' he said.

Another clatter of gunfire sounded, this time ripping into the wagons, but again thankfully all of it was too high to be effective.

'At least,' she said, 'most of them have poor aim.'

Jeff looked along the nearby ground, seeing no cover or any sign of where they could be holed up.

'They do, don't they?' Slowly Jeff raised his gaze from the ground to look at the dark form of the monolith. He saw speckles of light between the two fingers as another burst of gunfire tore into the wagon.

'They're on the rock,' Abigail said, following his gaze.

'Yeah,' Jeff murmured. 'And from up there they can keep us pinned down and pick us off as they choose.'

CHAPTER 12

'Stay here,' Cassidy said after listening to Jeff's explanation. 'I'll deal with them.'

Cassidy clasped Jeff's arm then crawled out from beneath the wagon.

Jeff watched him go, noting the cautious route he took. Then from his new vantage point with the main group, he appraised the boulders where the men they were trading gunfire with were hiding.

Over the next few minutes several men bobbed up and fired. Jeff counted only three opponents. That meant the convoy had superior numbers and without the wild gunfire from the rock they should prevail.

That thought made Jeff's mind up for him.

He crawled along beneath the lead wagon aiming to check on Abigail before he left, but before he reached her he saw her laying the still body of Todd on the ground.

He murmured a silent thanks to the plucky young lad who had saved his life then turned his attention to the men who had killed him. He crawled out from beneath the wagon and with his head down he set off after Cassidy.

He took the same route as Cassidy had along the length of the wagons on the blind side to the two-fingered rock. After passing Blake's body, he crawled out into open land, hoping the darkness and his slow movement would keep him hidden.

When he was fifty yards from the wagon he got to his feet and circled round to the rock. Although gunfire continued to rain down on the convey the darkness hid his progress and kept the gunfire away from him. Despite hurrying he didn't catch sight of Cassidy until he reached the scree.

Cassidy was halfway up the slope and climbing towards what was effectively a knuckle on the tallest finger of rock. He was out of view of the men firing down at the wagons, so Jeff followed him up, using the same route.

Cassidy didn't look down, being presumably unaware he was being followed, and he was reaching the top quickly. After already climbing the scree twice today Jeff was tired, but he had also worked out how to climb the shifting stones efficiently and so he gained on him.

Cassidy had reached the rock face and was working his way towards the gunmen when he glanced down for the first time. He gaze fell on Jeff, who stopped and raised his hands in case Cassidy didn't recognize him in the poor light.

Cassidy nodded and beckoned for him to join him, but then a gunshot pinged into the rocks at

Jeff's side. He swirled round and although he couldn't see who had fired, clearly someone had seen him.

A second and a third shot clattered into the rocks around him, forcing Jeff to hurry on, but he kicked off too quickly and dislodged a wide stretch of stones. That started a chain-reaction that shifted more stones at his feet. He went tumbling.

Unable to control himself he skidded down the scree, trying to find his footing on ground that wouldn't stay still. After tumbling for several seconds he decided his squirming was only making his predicament worse and so he resisted the urge to struggle. That let him slow to a halt, but when he looked up he was thirty yards further down the slope and worse, he'd slid diagonally and could now see the gunmen lined up between the rocks. And they were looking at him.

A line of guns levelled on him. Jeff threw himself on his chest as slugs whined and skittered over the rocks around him.

He was presenting a small profile and so with gritted teeth he forced himself not to panic and levelled his gun on the most prominent man. With his elbows planted firmly he picked out this man and fired.

His first shot was too high and his second was too low, but that helped him to judge the distance more accurately. With the man now in his sights his third shot hit its target and sent the man tumbling down the scree.

Returning gunfire clattered around him, but by then Cassidy had moved himself around the side of the rock. In a position where he wasn't visible to the gunmen, Cassidy picked off the nearest man. This man went falling head over heels while the other two men took flight and disappeared from sight between the rock fingers.

Cassidy hurried over the top of the scree, a hand trailing along the rock for balance, while Jeff jumped to his feet. As fast as he could he worked his way up the slope, this time taking a diagonal route towards the lawman.

Cassidy didn't slow his progress and when Jeff was still twenty yards behind him, he reached the corner. He risked looking around it then disappeared from view.

Twin gunshots exploded from within the two fingers of rock. Jeff hurried on, his gun trained on the gap between the rocks, but nobody showed.

No further gunshots had sounded when he reached the top. As he worked his way along the top of the scree, he glanced down at the wagons.

Sporadic gunfire was sounding down there and he could see men moving away from the wagon towards the boulders where the attackers had taken cover. Jeff reckoned this meant the defenders were getting the upper hand and that the Dark Riders here were amongst the last to be defeated.

He reached the corner and glanced between the rocks. The high and wide fingers of rock blocked off all light making the darkness almost tangible.

He jerked back in case his profile could be seen. Then, with his back pressed to the wall, he slipped around the corner. Despite straining his vision he could see nothing ahead except the starry sky framed in the gap between the fingers.

From somewhere strained breathing and scuffed footfalls sounded. Then he saw movement as two men shuffled into view.

He couldn't see who the two men were but they were struggling and that meant it had to be Cassidy and another man. He assumed the larger form was Cassidy's. He narrowed his eyes and was able to discern that Cassidy was holding the other man's shoulders and was trying to drag him down.

Jeff set off for them, but he'd managed only a few paces before his foot hit an object. He went down, sprawling over something that yielded beneath his hands and knees.

He placed a hand to the rock aiming to raise himself, but he felt dampness and his face rasped against cloth. He was lying on a body, he realized. He recoiled, but once he was back on his feet, he smiled as this meant the man Cassidy was fighting could be the last of the Dark Riders.

Jeff set off for them, recklessly running in the dark. As he approached he saw that they were on the edge of the rock where only a few hours earlier Samuel had fallen to his death. Cassidy was facing him with one heel on the very edge as the other man tried to push him over.

Jeff reached them. He wrapped an arm around the man's neck and tugged. Catching him unawares he was able to jerk the man away from Cassidy, but the sudden removal of his opponent made Cassidy lose his balance. He fell to his knees, waving his arms as he sought his balance on the edge.

With the man digging in a heel then turning his attention towards pushing Jeff over the side, Jeff had to put Cassidy from his mind. He struggled and turned as he strained to pull the man down. In the darkness Jeff couldn't see the man's face but he could hear his hoarse breathing. He also couldn't tell how near the edge he was, only his inability to see the sky letting him work out that he now had his back to the edge.

Then his back foot gave way.

He kicked out, searching for solid rock, but his foot found only air. He fell. His knee jarred on the very edge of the rock, sending numbing pain through his leg. Then his other leg slipped over the edge and his hold of the man's neck came away.

With his belly pressed to the edge and his feet dangling, he looked up. He saw the outline of an arm thrusting towards his chest, aiming to tip him over the side, but as the open palm slapped his shoulder and pushed him away, a second arm darted across his vision. Cassidy's fist connected with the man's head, sending him reeling.

Jeff slapped both hands to the rock to try to stop his motion, but the rock was smooth and slick. Slowly he slipped backwards. He wheeled his legs, but could find no purchase on the sheer rock.

As his hold on the edge slipped away, the large silhouette of Cassidy battered the man one way then the other, all the time forcing him to back away.

Then, with a round-arm punch to the man's jaw, Cassidy sent his assailant spinning away from view over the edge. Jeff avoided looking down and following his progress, knowing that the movement would only make him join him.

A prolonged scream sounded, but before it cut off Cassidy was standing over him and, as Jeff's own hold of the rock snapped away, a hand slapped down on his arm, halting him.

'I've sent two bad men over the edge today,' Cassidy said, tugging Jeff back up on to the rock. 'It's about time I brought a good man back.'

'You're letting me stay free?' Jeff asked, now that the convoy was ready to move out and Cassidy was still showing no sign of cuffing him.

'More than that,' Cassidy said. 'I'm letting you go free. You can stay with the convoy or leave with Abigail, the choice is yours.'

'Why? I still did wrong.'

Cassidy smiled. 'Trying to talk me out of it proves I'm doing the right thing. But if you need an answer, last night you saved my life, amongst many. Your actions more than repaid whatever mistakes you made.'

'But I didn't save everyone,' Jeff said, remembering the grave he'd hated digging the most.

Last night they'd lost only two men, a heartening success when dealing with the ruthless Dark Riders who had wiped out a whole settlement and the previous convoy, but those two had included Todd.

'I know,' Cassidy said. 'One young man did everything right and another young man did everything wrong.'

'Does that mean you've decided what you'll tell Samuel's father?'

Cassidy sighed. 'I considered claiming that Todd's demise was the way Samuel died, hoping that would soften the blow, but I won't. Neither of them deserve to be remembered falsely. So I'll tell him the truth, no matter how painful that is for him, and me.'

'If there's one thing I've learnt over the last few weeks, it's that the truth is always for the best.'

As Cassidy nodded, Jeff looked at Abigail, who was ready to move out. She was eyeing this conversation with interest, but she was smiling, suggesting Cassidy had already told her that he was letting him go.

'Which is why I feel so sad for her,' Cassidy said, joining him in looking at her. 'Her search for Jane is hopeless. You know that, don't you?'

Jeff considered telling Cassidy the information with which Blake had bought his loyalty. In his jacket was a locket Blake had found amongst the bones. It contained a picture of a woman whose features resembled Abigail's and which carried an inscription from someone called Ethan.

'Yeah,' he said, deciding that Abigail had to be the first person to see it. 'The bones up there probably were her sister's, but she needs to search some more before she'll accept that. When the time is right, I'll persuade her to give up.'

'Then I wish you luck, whatever you find.'

'And you.'

Cassidy nodded then headed away. Jeff watched him get up on the lead wagon and beckon for everyone to begin the long trek to Bleak Point and an encounter that was sure to be tough. Then he joined Abigail. Without discussion they mounted up and turned away from the two-fingered rock.

With the morning sun on their backs they set off for the fourth and final cross on the map, a three-day journey.

'What do we do if we find nothing there?' Abigail asked when the convoy was just a distant mark on the horizon.

'We'll see the miners at Bleak Point,' Jeff said, 'check out other landmarks, explore beyond the Barren Plains, and keep on searching until we find her.'

'And if we still don't find her then?'

Jeff shrugged, the action pressing the locket against his chest.

'Then we'll return here to look at the bones again and search around more thoroughly. Perhaps we might have missed something.'

'Perhaps we might have,' she said, although she didn't sound hopeful. 'Or perhaps I might be prepared to hear the truth by then. Until then, if you don't mind staying with me, I want to keep her dream alive of putting down roots somewhere out here.'

'The only thing I'm looking forward to in this

quest is staying with you.' Jeff turned to her and offered a smile. 'And remember, there's another way you can keep her dream alive.'

She returned a warming smile. 'I know that, but later. . . .'

Jeff reckoned that promise was good enough for him.

'Yes,' he said. 'Later.'